THRILL OF THE GAME

LUST FOR THREE

HELANA PARKINS

plicit Press

CHAPTER 1

CHANCE ENCOUNTER: THE THRILL OF THE GAME BOOK 1

SANDRA FROWNED as she stared into the mirror, pulling the brush methodically through her long, light brown hair. Was that a new wrinkle at the corner of her mouth? She couldn't be sure.

The routine of her morning ablutions was so familiar, totally unchanged as it had been for four or five years, that it was in a dazed stupor that she continued preparing herself for work; devoid of all thought save the niggling worry about the wrinkle. Even this was not bothering her too much.

'After all,' she thought with a grim sigh, 'it's not as though Chad even cares about my appearance much these days. And he's the only one who will notice it...'

Chad was downstairs, but he had already finished his breakfast by the time she began hers. Back when they had first married they had always made a point of eating together in the mornings: it was a bonding activity, which they both enjoyed. These days, however, they were so busy with their work and their individual schedules that the tradition had disappeared.

As she sat sipping her coffee, she told herself she didn't

care. All marriages began settling down after a while, didn't they? And anyway, she and Chad could be in a worse situation. She was sure that he had never cheated on her, and they very rarely argued. True, even though they were living together, their actual conversations were quite a few; but she was pretty certain that this happened to all couples sooner or later.

She could hear Chad moving around now, rustling by the mirror in the hallway. She knew without looking that he was adjusting his tie in the mirror; she could tell from the faint grunts of concentration he was emitting as he strove to get the knot just right. The noises he made used to endear him to her; even something as mundane as the task he was engaged in now could make her think of their times romping together. It had been a long time since he had been able to elicit such excitement from her, though. Listening to him now, the only thing she felt was a faint disgust. So wrapped up was she in these thoughts that she barely acknowledged his 'See you later, honey,' as he stepped out the door. The click of the door brought her back to now, and she turned to her muesli, blinking sadly.

Yes, she was pretty certain the spark going out of their relationship was just an inevitable part of getting older...

She often found herself 'waking up, as it were, halfway through her walk to work, with no recollection of leaving the house. This happened today as she strolled down the quiet streets, gazing blankly at the rows of identical houses and their neat, well-kept front yards.

Today, however, there seemed to be something about the freshness of the air which caused her to begin paying more attention to the scenery as she strode past; something which for some surprising reason was making her smile.

The summer was fast approaching with its stifling heat,

but for now, the air remained crisp and cool, and she felt her hair being lifted slightly by the breeze blowing in from the lake just outside town. Looking up, she noticed the view of the mountains, visible at the end of the street she had just turned to walk down; blue and mysterious in the morning mist.

Sandra saw those mountains every day and took them in without a second thought, but today she was suddenly struck by how beautiful their hazy outlines appeared; so much so that she actually stopped in the middle of the street to take in the sight. As she did so, the breeze playfully lifted up her blouse, fluttering the garment against her torso and briefly exposing her breasts. She giggled, smoothing it down and glancing around in embarrassment; but the street was almost empty and the few people there were busy hurrying to work, and hadn't noticed.

Even so, Sandra could not help but be filled with an illicit thrill at the incident, which remained with her as she entered the large complex of buildings where her office was and began making her way towards the elevator.

Somehow the freshness of the morning and the strange mood she was in were combining to mean that instead of the usual grim preparation for a dull day, she was filling inexorably with alluring emotions. It was more than a little odd; as she stepped into the elevator she wondered vaguely if she might be coming down with some kind of illness. The feeling was not unpleasant, though; on the contrary, she felt more alive than she had in a long time.

As the sturdy, timeworn elevator began laboriously climbing the six floors to her office it occurred to Sandra that the strange feelings could have something to do with a deficit in her sex life. She and Chad were still sleeping together, although she could not remember off-hand when the last time they had sex had been, and as for the last *good* time, well...

This thought alone was enough to create a strong surge of both frustration and longing within her; so powerful she almost gasped aloud. Looking up, however, she noticed for the first time that she was not alone in the elevator, and she stood up straight, hurriedly trying to control her emotions as she peered surreptitiously at the elevator's other occupant to make sure she had not been acting too noticeably weird.

Luckily, the other person was looking intently at their mobile phone and Sandra breathed an inward sigh of relief. She hated seeing even a little out of the ordinary in public, and it was especially unthinkable during work hours. Her firm was highly respected and its name is known by everyone in town; it would never do to appear anything other than completely professional in connection with them.

The elevator was an old one; everyone in the building had been complaining for months that it needed replacing, but so far no one had gotten around to it. Today the journey to the sixth floor felt as though it was taking even longer than usual, and to pass the time Sandra stole another glance at her traveling companion; finding herself intrigued by their appearance.

She was a woman; a stranger who Sandra had never seen before in this building. At a guess, Sandra thought she was probably about two decades younger than herself; in her early twenties, or twenty-five at most, and as Sandra's eyes passed in idle interest over her figure Sandra could not help but be struck by the brightness of her blue eyes, compared to the deep brown of her sun-kissed skin.

As Sandra looked at her, the woman glanced up, meeting her gaze with those sapphire-blue eyes. Now that she was looking directly at her Sandra was even more impressed with the sheer beauty and clarity of them; so much so that for a good second she simply gazed back, reeling slightly from the force of this stranger's loveliness.

Suddenly she noticed how rude she was being, and dropped her gaze hurriedly. To her surprise, however, the beautiful stranger seemed totally unperturbed. "Taking a long time, isn't it?" she commented mildly.

Sandra looked up, meeting again those gorgeous eyes, and saw to her relief that the woman was smiling; a warm radiant grin, which instantly put her at her ease. "It's an old elevator," she explained. "We've been trying to get the super to replace it, but..." she shrugged helplessly, smiling.

"Right," said the stranger, laughing as she tossed back her dark shining hair from her face. "I know how it is!"

"Exactly," agreed Sandra amicably. "It's just..." She broke off, giving an abrupt yelp and flinging her arm out wildly to stop herself from falling to the floor as the elevator gave a sudden, sickening jerk.

The stranger yelled as well, and they both gasped in panic as the whole container lurched wildly and the lights flickered off. "What the...!" cried both women, groping around in the darkness.

"What's happening?!" cried the stranger, as Sandra tried to work out which way was up.

She thought she was lying on top of the stranger, but she couldn't be sure. Just then, the lights came back on. Somehow they had both ended up in a heap on the floor, and Sandra realized that she was gripping the stranger's arms with some force.

Struggling backward, she relinquished her hold. "Sorry about that," she said, "I guess I got a little scared..."

"That's ok!" replied the other woman, shifting around

to try to get up. In doing so, she brought her torso right up to Sandra's head, and Sandra found herself suddenly gazing into a pair of firm, rounded, honey-colored breasts, only just concealed by the woman's low-cut and tight-fitting blacktop.

She had seen many breasts before, of course; but being in such close proximity to such beautiful ones, when she was in such a strange mood already, was really making her feel funny. She found that her breathing had become shallow; her pussy began tingling with an insistent desire, such as she had not felt for Chad for many years.

" Oh! Sorry," said the stranger, moving back and getting gracefully to her feet, "Here, let me help you up."

"Thanks," said Sandra, taking the dainty brown hand that was offered to her, and managing with some effort to control her breathing as the woman assisted her to her feet.

"I think the elevator got stuck," commented the stranger lightly, once both were standing again.

Sandra, who was still experiencing a lot of inner turmoil regarding her feelings for this vision, took the news with incredulity. "No way," she said, stepping forwards to the door and firmly pressing the 'open' button. Her action elicited no response, and Sandra, still incredulous, began heaving at the huge steel slab of the door itself. "What! It's true!" she gasped, as she found this also yielding no results. "What are we going to do?"

Her companion shrugged, looking earnestly at her with those fantastic, sparkling eyes. Sandra noticed that amongst the deep sea-blue her eyes had little flecks of golden brown, and found herself staring helplessly into them, as though pulled by a deep and throbbing attraction...

"I'm sure it'll be ok though," the girl said, smiling radiantly again and snapping Sandra out of her reverie. "All we have to do is push the 'alarm' button, and they'll come to get us in no time!"

As she said this she reached past Sandra to the red button on the wall of the elevator, giving Sandra a waft of her sweet, dark scent as she did so. "Hey, uh...are you alright?" the girl asked.

Sandra opened her eyes, noticing for the first time that she had closed them in longing. The stranger was looking at her with such intense concern that for a split second, Sandra seriously felt as though she were falling in love. Then the moment passed, however, and she pulled herself together. "Just a little shaken," she said, standing up straighter. "I've never been stuck in an elevator before."

"Me neither," replied her companion. "It's not as bad as I imagined, though. Especially as I'm not on my own..."

"That would be worse," agreed Sandra.

"Are you sure you're ok, though?" continued the girl. "You look awfully pale. Maybe you should take off your jacket? It's getting a little stuffy." As she said this, she began peeling off her own jacket, somehow in doing so moving closer to Sandra so that the sweet curve of her breasts was fully visible again. Hurriedly, Sandra pulled off her own jacket, noticing as she did so that she had begun perspiring heavily.

The gorgeous stranger sat down on the floor of the elevator, apparently ready to settle down in comfort as they waited for assistance. Tentatively, Sandra sat beside her, still more than a little confused by the swirl of emotions rushing through her. Was she just imagining it, or was the stranger glancing at her with the same inexplicable lust that Sandra herself was feeling? She could not imagine why, yet as she looked up at the girl's face she saw her clearly licking her lips in what seemed a distinctly amorous manner.

The girl sighed, flinging her arm up fitfully and stretch-ing, then bringing it down again. As she did so she lightly brushed Sandra's thigh, and Sandra looked up, confusion coursing through her. Was she right in thinking this girl was giving the same signals? As she once again met those glit-tering eyes with hers, she became sure. The woman beside her was looking at her with unmistakable lust.

In any other situation, such a fiery gaze would have turned Sandra right off; but here and now it was all she wanted. And what a perfect setting; stuck here together, they could do whatever they wanted, and no one would ever be the wiser...

Just then the door opened with a crashing thud, and both women leaped up, the sizzle of chemistry abruptly broken.

A worried-looking man was standing before them, hatchet in hand as he prized the door fully apart. "You ladies ok?"

"Fine, fine," replied the stranger. "Thank you sooo much!" Daintily, she stepped out of the wreck of the eleva-tor, and without a backward glance at Sandra, skipped lightly away.

Over the next few days, Sandra found herself puzzling over the incident with increasing frequency. It was not so much the woman's abrupt exit that she had minded; if it was true that the stranger had felt the same lust as Sandra had, then Sandra was not at all sure she could have gone through with anything for real. No, it was Sandra's horniness itself that was baffling her. Though she didn't get the same feel-ings for any more women after the elevator, she had to admit that something inside her had changed fundamen-tally that day.

She had been more or less content with her job; but

now she found herself being interrupted by frequent daydreams at her desk, to the point where her colleagues began commenting on her absent-mindedness. What was weirder was that she did not seem able to care that much. It was very odd, and she would have liked very much to confide in someone about the change. Every time she was alone with Chad, however, it never seemed to be the right opportunity. There was always something to do; either the recycling needed to be taken out, or dinner had to be made, or some other task which she had previously regarded as important but which was now seeming somehow trivial.

Three days after the meeting in the elevator, she arrived home from work in a more confused state than ever. The sun was just setting and the whole neighborhood was glowing in the soft evening breeze, and as she stepped inside she strode purposefully towards the lounge, determined today to actually share her feelings with Chad, such as she could explain them. She knew that tonight there were no pressing household tasks that needed doing, and so she strode purposefully into the lounge, saying eagerly, "It's a lovely evening; let's go out for a walk!"

The idea seemed so right to her that it had not occurred to her that Chad may disagree, so she was completely nonplussed to find him engrossed in a TV show of some kind, dismissing her suggestion with a vague wave of the hand.

"Come on!" she cried, stepping in front of the screen and gazing imploringly at him.

Chad sighed, moving his head slightly to try to catch what the person on the TV was saying. Didn't Sandra understand that he had had a long and tiring day, and he needed to unwind?

"Why don't you want to?" asked his wife, and he glanced at her.

There seemed to be something a little volatile in her deep hazel eyes tonight; something he did not altogether understand, and which he felt in no way equipped to deal with.

"Too tired. Where would we walk to anyway?" he asked with a shrug.

Sandra stared down at him, barely able to contain her fury. Chad was looking past her again, craning his neck around to try to see behind her; succeeding pretty well in acting as though she were merely a slightly inconvenient obstacle to his screen time.

Suddenly it felt as though they had not even properly looked at each other for days and days; weeks or months even, and Chad's placid dismissal began becoming almost too much to bear.

"How long have you been sitting there, just staring at this, this, bullshit?" she demanded, stepping closer to him and bringing her face towards his.

Chad stared at her, surprised at the ferocity of her tone; he sat up, bristling defensively.

"For your information, I only got in about ten minutes ago!" he cried, in a strident tone, which Sandra rarely heard him use these days, and with which many years ago he could use to make her swoon at his confidence.

Now, however, it only served to annoy her more, and she spat in reply, "And you'd rather just sit there wasting your life away than spend quality time with me?"

"Oh I like that!" he retorted, "Why would I want to spend quality time with you when all I get is abuse?"

"What's so abusive about wanting to go for a walk with you?" she cried, trying and failing to keep her voice steady.

"If you're so keen to walk, just get out my way and *walk*, why don't you?" he replied, glaring at her with a fury which, painful though it was, somehow also thrilled her with passion.

It had been a long time since she'd seen him so emotional.

She could not relent now though after he had been so rude to her; she had her pride, after all. So, with what she hoped was an icy glare, she snapped, "Fine," and swept out of the house, walking quickly to suppress the scream of frustration burning within her.

She was so angry that it was some time before she noticed how far she had walked. She and Chad lived in a neat suburban development on the outskirts of town, and Sandra realized now just how close to the edge of town it was. Already she had reached scrubby grassland and stretching before her, about half a mile away, lay the majestic expanse of the lake, twinkling rosily in the fading light. Just visible was the edge of the huge dam, which created the lake in the first place; its white face glowing now a deep orange-gold, and turning around, Sandra gasped as she saw the last of the evening sunlight fading with burning splendor from the sky over the town behind her.

Turning back to the lake, she found herself sighing with a new calmness. She had forgotten how close she lived to such a wondrous natural beauty; as swiftly as she had managed to reach this viewpoint tonight, she could not remember the last time she had come to this place. It had just never seemed that important before. The lake was there and had been for her entire life.

She stayed gazing at the view for some time, while the sky deepened to a royal blue and the lights of the dam began twinkling quietly in the clear air. Then, with a soft sigh, she made her way back home, returning to the house in a pleasantly contemplative mood. 'It doesn't matter how Chad is acting,' she thought as she pushed her key into the door. 'I'm sure he had his reasons, and we can work out whatever problems we have...'

So sure of this was she that she pushed open the lounge door in total confidence that she would be received well, even though the TV was still blaring from inside.

Sitting beside Chad, she turned to look at him, compassion filling her as she gazed at his tousled chocolate-colored hair and pale, chiseled features, glowing faintly in the blue light of the screen.

"Hi," he muttered, giving her a cursory glance before turning his attention back to the program. Undeterred, she stroked his arm, murmuring, "Sorry about earlier. I know how much you like to relax after work."

"Oh," he said. "That's ok, don't worry about it."

Softly, she moved closer to him, basking in the warmth of his body, "You know, if we go up to the bedroom, we might find some even better ways of relaxing," she added, moving her arm up to lightly run her fingers down his clean-shaven cheek.

"Mmm," he said, encouragingly, and she began moving her hand down, caressing his chest and belly. "I'm just going to watch the last five minutes of this," he said, turning to gaze at her. "I'll be right up."

She pouted, unsatisfied. "You sure?" "Promise," he insisted, and so, in a state of some excitement, she made her way up to their room.

Five minutes passed, then ten; and still no Chad. Still, she was feeling more desire for him than she had for many months, and eagerly, she changed into one of her sexiest nightgowns. Then she lay down in bed to wait for her husband.

She awoke alone, with her hand on her groin and her thoughts confused. Sitting up, she realized two things: that she was more turned on than she had been for a very long time, and that Chad had taken so long the previous night that she had fallen asleep before he got there. And where was he now?

She pulled herself upright and listened carefully. Yes, he was still here: that was him clattering around downstairs. He never was very good at doing things quietly, regardless of other people sleeping. Sandra was highly tempted to confront him dressed as she was in her skimpy lace nightgown, but the bedside clock showed clearly that there was no time for this. So, sighing, she pulled on instead a work suit and made her way downstairs.

Chad heard her coming down with some trepidation. He was certain last night was not his fault: he had ended up crashing out in front of the TV and did not wake up until that morning. In fact, he was running late as it was; he just did not have time to explain anything to Sandra...

"So...what happened last night?"

She had slid gracefully into the kitchen unexpectedly and was gazing at him with those bright hazel eyes whose intensity he had used to adore getting lost in, but which now were simply too much for him.

"Nothing," he said, looking away. "I just fell asleep downstairs."

She tried to question him more, but there was something about her manner that was slightly alarming; she seemed more emotional than she had in a long time, and he did not feel in any way equipped to deal with it. "I've got to go," he explained, sweeping past her out of the kitchen; leaving Sandra frozen in thin-lipped frustration.

Over the next week or so, their exchanges became more and more fraught with tension, until Sandra began feeling as though she could not say anything to Chad, which did not end up upsetting him. In a way, Chad knew he was being awkward; rather than address their issues, he preferred always to brush the argument aside, and although he frequently had the niggling feeling that this was only exacerbating the problem, his natural dislike of confrontations meant he was unwilling to change.

For Sandra's part, she would have greatly preferred if Chad did shout at her, instead of just acting as though she was being melodramatic. She still had not shared her frustrations with him or her newly awakened sexual curiosity, and as the days wore on she began becoming increasingly agitated.

It did not help that both their workloads had increased, and so as well as the constant bickering and frosty silences, they were both showing signs of tension from lack of sleep.

It was after a particularly short night, which Sandra had spent dreaming uneasily of her clients, that she came down and greeted Chad, to receive absolutely nothing in response: her husband did not even lift up his head from his cereal.

Staring at him sitting there in such obstinate oblivion, she felt the rage building up inside her. Suddenly everything was totally unclouded: she did not have to deal with any of this anymore.

The realization was such a relief that she almost felt the anger receding. She was still annoyed enough for Chad to sense the seriousness of her decision, however; as she smacked her hand on the table in front of him and snapped, "This has to end, now! You're not being fair!"

He looked up, startled; and seeing the fury in her eyes, something inside him snapped as well. "*I'm* not being fair? Why would I want to speak to you when every word you've said to me for the past week has been accusatory?"

"Maybe you need to think about changing your behavior, if I am accusing you of so much," she retorted, realizing that her courtroom talk was coming out but barely caring as she stepped closer to Chad, standing over him as she said, "It's not fair that I should have to come back from a hard day at the office to zero support from my husband" –

"Well how do you think *I* feel?" he cut in; part of him hating himself for his whining tone, but unable to stop it, "You haven't exactly been acting like a loving wife lately."

"I would if you'd let me, Chad!" she cried, seeing an opening here, but he was still alarmed by her aggressive manner, and standing up, he made to leave the kitchen.

This was too much for Sandra. Moving swiftly, she stood in front of him, drawing herself up to her full height to glare at him; though even with her high-heeled work shoes she was still a good inch or so shorter than him. "That's not good enough," she said, surprised at how calm and sure her voice suddenly was; "Not anymore. If we can't even be in the same room together, maybe we need to think about some kind of change."

"What?" asked Chad, surprised, and she saw to her relief that she appeared to have finally got through to him.

"I'm serious, Chad," she said.

"Are you saying you want a divorce?" he replied, sitting down heavily and staring at her with a sudden pleading look which at that moment she found totally disgusting.

"It doesn't have to be so drastic," she said, "But can't you see we can't go on like this?"

He shrugged, infuriating her again, and she cried, "Well anyway, I can't go on like this! And if you aren't willing to communicate we need to get someone to help us!"

Chad wrinkled his nose. "You mean like marriage counseling?" he asked unenthusiastically, and she nodded. "But can't we just" –

"No," replied Sandra, suddenly very wary of all the games. "Either we get counseling, or we really go on a break. It's your choice, Chad – you've heard what I have to say."

"But" –

"I have to get to work," she cut in, "I expect you to have decided by tonight".

She hurried out of the kitchen, half scared that he would say something to melt the icy sensation in her heart; half wishing that he would. But he said nothing as she exited, save a bitter comment as she was already halfway up the stairs: "You're just doing now what you were calling unfair in me!"

She shook her head sadly as she continued up the stairs. She didn't know if counseling would be enough to save them.

Chad spent a moody day at the office, with the result that by the afternoon he had a huge pile of reports to go through and absolutely no gumption to do them. Chris, his partner in the office, noticed him sighing in frustration. "Hey, why don't you take tomorrow morning off to do them?" he suggested, "I can man the office until the afternoon when the new data comes in. And maybe you'll get more done at home where you can relax a little."

"I'm not sure about relaxing," muttered Chad; but he agreed to take Chris' advice. Sandra would not be in all morning, after all; and maybe it would do him good to have the house to himself for a little while.

So pleased was he with the prospect, that as soon as he got home he promised Sandra with as much enthusiasm as he could muster that the counseling was a good idea, though privately he didn't see how sitting in front of a stranger dissecting their problems could possibly help to resolve them. As Sandra left the room to make the appointment, he added under his breath, "Not that it will do any good."

The next day he had already risen, dressed, and break-fasted before he recalled that he did not have to be at the office until after lunch. The sun was glinting greenly into the kitchen through the bright, lush leaves of the acacia trees outside, and the whole house was more peaceful than it had been for a very long time. As he considered this he got a twinge of sadness; he should not feel better in his shared home when the woman he was supposed to love was not there. Of late, however, he was having difficulty remem-bering exactly what it was about her that caused him to love her anyway.

Pushing these difficult thoughts aside, he decided to take a stroll down to the store. The oppressive summer heat was on its way, but today the cool breeze from the lake miti-gated the harsh glare of the sun; a breeze, which in a few weeks' time as the desert beyond the lake heated up, would change from refreshing to brutally hot. For now, though, Chad could enjoy it, and so he walked unhurriedly the four or five blocks to the store.

He had been planning to simply stock up on a few essential items and maybe get ice cream in honor of the summery weather, but as he wandered around the store he found himself enjoying being one of the only people there once that he found himself dawdling, looking at everything that took his fancy. So relaxed was he feeling that he even stopped at the noticeboard, perusing the adverts and announcements with a distinct feeling of leisure.

He was not actually looking for anything; though some of the notices were pretty amusing.

"Such a strange glimpse into other peoples' lives in this town," he murmured, as he passed his eye over the prolifera-tion of cards; some scrawled hastily in clumsy handwriting, others neatly typed with intriguing pictures.

As he looked down at the leaflets spread on the table in front of the noticeboard, one of these pictures, in particular, happened to catch his eye.

It was a business card; and the picture was quite a simple one really: just a photo of the head and shoulders of a girl, her long blonde hair falling about her round face. She was gazing out of the card with a strangely alluring smile; a smile that seemed to melt all of Chad's worries away. Intrigued, he picked one of the cards up, his eyes widening as he read the tagline.

"Need to spice up your relationship? Call Desiree." There was nothing else except a phone number. Excitedly, Chad pocketed the card and hurried out of the store, muttering, "It can't be a coincidence!"

The good mood produced by the discovery of the card lasted all day, and it was not until Chad was on his way home that he began to have doubts about what he would tell Sandra. He needed to come up with a plausible reason why he had suddenly decided to abandon the counseling idea, but what?

So deep was the mistrust that the couple held each other in by this point that it did not even occur to him to tell Sandra the truth and show her the card. But he could not help looking at it, sitting at the kitchen table gazing at the helpful, smiling face of the mysterious woman, and it was in this position that Sandra walked in on him as she came back from work.

Instantly Chad jumped up, attempting to hide the card in his pocket, but managing instead to drop it on the floor.

"What is that?" asked Sandra curiously.

"Nothing!" he cried; far too defensively, and, her interest piqued, she dived to the floor, snatching up the card before he had time to stop her. Chad groaned, re-taking his seat and putting his head in his hands. How was he going to explain this one? Sandra's tone of voice caused him to look up again. For the first time in what felt like years, she was speaking to him not with anger, distaste, or accusation; but with honest frankness. "Were you thinking about calling this girl?"

He peered at her, wondering at first whether or not the new tone was some kind of trick. She was gazing at him openly, however; and he thought he could even detect a slight smile around the corners of her mouth. "Do you... want to?" he asked.

Sandra studied the card again. She could not explain why, but she felt inexorably attracted to the blonde, smiling woman. The feeling was as powerful as the desire she had felt for the stranger in the elevator; yet it was different, as well. It was not lust she felt for this Desiree; "She looks like she can help us," she said simply.

So charged were they with the strange energy produced by the card that they agreed that Sandra should call the number immediately. Desiree answered on the third ring. "How can I help you?"

"Uh..." Sandra, whose very profession relied on her proficiency with words, was for the moment at a loss for them. The warm, lilting voice on the other end of the line cut into her thoughts, putting her at her ease. "Are you a couple looking for some...spice?"

"Well, yes, I suppose we are, yes," agreed Sandra, liking her already. Desiree suggested that they meet up that very night; in a bar, which Sandra thought a little odd, but which Chad was pleased about.

"Shows she knows it's nice and casual," he said, as they walked out of the house together into the golden evening. As they arrived at the bar Sandra glanced up at Chad beside her; at his face, today so blissfully free of worry. Spontaneously, she laughed aloud, taking his hand. It was almost worth coming out just for this, and they had not even met Desiree yet...

The long, wooden building of the bar was packed with merry groups of people, and at first Sandra and Chad squeezed through them a little lost, craning their necks all around. Neither had been in a social situation for so long that both had to remember how to act, and their self-consciousness meant that they automatically pressed closer to each other as they made their way through the throng.

"Well, you don't seem like your relationship is in too much trouble," commented a warm voice, and they looked around, instantly recognizing the long, flowing blonde hair and glinting blue eyes of the photo. "How did you know it was us?" asked Sandra incredulously, as the young lady skipped up to them, kissing them each on the cheek in greeting.

Her lips were soft, and Sandra felt strange tingles traveling through her at their touch that she was not entirely sure how to react to. Desiree was already leading them over to the bar, however, and she pushed the sensation aside as they got drinks and then, on Desiree's suggestion, made their way outside into the garden where they found an empty table with relative ease.

Though the garden was less crowded than inside the bar, the benches under the fairy-light-strung trees were full enough that the three had to sit close together in order to hear themselves talk. At first, Desiree simply asked some introductory questions, nodding so enthusiastically that both Chad and Sandra felt themselves instantly drawn to her.

Desiree was older than she had looked in her photo, though it was difficult to say how old. At times she would laugh so sweetly and glance at the couple so innocently that she looked scarcely above eighteen, and at times she would come out with comments so wise Sandra felt she was talking to someone with at least as much world experience as she. For sure, Desiree was at least ten years younger than Sandra, and the older woman felt herself becoming infused with excitement at Desiree's energy. Glancing at Chad as they chatted away, she could see he felt it too.

Somehow the drinks kept on flowing; though as there never seemed to be a pause in the conversation, it was difficult to see how. Sandra was beginning to feel tipsy, but she was enjoying herself so much that she embraced the sensation willingly. Desiree was chattering away again; she seemed equally comfortable with talking as with listening intently to whatever Chad and Sandra had to contribute. Right now she was enthusing about the part of town where the Joneses lived. "Oh, you guys are really close to the lake!" she cried, eyes shining in delight. "That must be amazing!"

"It is," agreed Sandra and Chad, catching each other's eyes and smiling at their speaking together.

"We don't always appreciate it, though," added Chad, surprising Sandra with the sincerity of his tone.

"Oh I know, right?" agreed Desiree. "It's just one of those places you go so much as a kid that you just assume it's always going to be there. Then one day you notice you only ever think about the things you used to do there. I remember when we used to go skinny dipping there every night..." She broke off, gazing wistfully into the distance.

"I haven't done that for a long, long time," commented Chad softly, and Sandra noticed with some interest that both he and herself had been holding their breath, as if in anticipation.

"No..." agreed Sandra, and the three were silent for a couple of beats.

Then Desiree picked up her glass, sipping from it and glancing importantly up at the couple before her.

Sensing that she was about to say something significant, they both leaned forwards instinctively. "I suppose you want to know more about my methods," she commented, gazing at them. They glanced at each other, each seeing the same excitement that they felt reflected in the other's eyes. "Yes," agreed Sandra. "What do you mean by 'spicing up'?"

Desiree giggled; her small, round breasts shaking in a way, which filled both of the Joneses with unprecedented desire, though they were careful not to show this to each other. "Well it's more about what you mean, I suppose," she said mysteriously. "I'm only really here to help you achieve what you want."

"But what do you mean by that?" asked Chad, and Desiree looked at him steadily, giving him a saucy wink, which sent instant messages to his groin.

"Whatever you want to do, I'll help you do it," she said, giggling again.

Sandra and Chad looked at each other, nonplussed: neither having the faintest idea what she was talking about.

"Well, in that case, it must be time for another drink!" said Chad, to hide his confusion, and the two women raised their empty glasses in agreement.

As he wandered off to the bar, Desiree leaned forwards, gazing earnestly into Sandra's eyes. "It's very kind of you to do this for us," murmured Sandra, mainly to have something to say to distract herself from the butterflies that had unaccountably begun fluttering inside her.

"Don't say that," replied Desiree. "I like you and Chad already. And I'm sure I'll enjoy helping you just as much as you do...."

"I still don't exactly know what you mean about helping us," admitted Sandra.

"Well, it depends on your preference and style, of course," replied the younger woman. "But you guys seem ready for an adventure, so why not?"

"Why not what?" inquired Chad, placing a tray with their new drinks on the table. Desiree took hers, sipping it slowly and licking her full, pink lips as she gazed from one to the other of the couple before her.

"You guys are finding the spark is going out of your relationship, right?" she asked. Both nodded, frowning slightly as they tried to work out where this was headed. "Well, what better way to rekindle it," continued Desiree, "than in the bedroom?"

She leaned forward even further; so close that her face was almost touching those of Chad and Sandra. They stared at her, each beginning to feel a slow and illicit throbbing in their veins. "I'm still not sure I quite understand," said Sandra; for some reason her voice coming out in a husky whisper.

Desiree turned to her, parting her lips. "I mean, I can

help you both explore sexually," she said frankly, her eyes flicking up and down Sandra's torso.

"Are you saying, you want us to all...sleep...together?" asked Sandra. Desiree's gaze flicked to Chad, checking his response; then she nodded firmly. Sandra and Chad sat still for a moment as this totally unexpected suggestion sunk in. Then both sat back, laughing as they looked at each other and shaking their heads.

"No way!" cried Chad; though Desiree's mere words had been enough to mean that he had to cross his legs to hide his body's reaction to the idea.

Sandra agreed, equally unconvincingly, "I mean, we've never done anything like that before!"

'But I'd love to try,' she thought; though she pushed it away. Surely the addition of a whole new lover into an already fractious relationship was bound to cause more tension, not less?

"Oh, don't worry about *that*," insisted Desiree, gazing at them wide-eyed. "I've never done anything like it, really, before, either. As a matter of fact, I'm pretty inexperienced when it comes to sex!" She giggled, again endearing herself inexorably to both Sandra and Chad.

"But then...how would we do it?" asked the latter. Desiree shrugged, her smile changing from innocent to saucy with breathtaking rapidity.

"We'll just try," she said simply. "What's wrong with a little...experimentation?"

As Desiree left to visit the bathroom, Sandra and Chad put their heads together, each almost bursting with excitement but each trying to hide it from the other. "It's crazy, right?" asked Chad. "We should just forget the whole thing, right?"

'Because otherwise, you will be madly jealous of Desiree

and I,' he added; although only in his head. Sandra looked at him, noticing for the first time the gleam in his dark brown eyes. Suddenly all the weeks and months of heartache and frustration came back to her, and all at once, she decided that anything would be better than staying in that situation; no matter how outlandish it seemed.

"Why don't we go for it?" she asked.

"Really?" replied Chad, eyes widening. Sandra had not seen him so excited in so long that she felt anything would be worth it to keep those dark eyes gleaming with the happiness she had half feared was gone forever.

"We're already feeling closer than we have in months," she pointed out, "Imagine how much better it could be if we actually go through with what Desiree's suggesting?" She looked into his eyes, seeing to her utter delight his mouth curling into a slow, mischievous grin.

"So shall we invite her back to our place?" he inquired. She gasped. "Tonight?"

"No time like the present," said a soft, lilting voice, and they turned to see Desiree standing beside them, her entire body radiating pleasure and the promise of more.

"Let's go," agreed Sandra, trying to keep her voice steady as she felt her heartbeat increase.

CHAPTER 2

LUST FOR THREE: THE THRILL OF THE GAME BOOK 2

SANDRA GAZED AROUND HER, the three or four drinks she had consumed at the bar giving a pleasantly fuzzy glow to the familiar room; as well as to the two other people in it. She still could not quite believe what was happening, and the whole evening seemed to be some kind of sweet and subtle dream: the illicit conversations in the bar, the pounding of her heart in the taxi home, the flurry of giggling conversations as she and Chad clumsily welcomed Desiree to their house, the increasingly flirtatious tone of which had led, without Sandra being sure exactly how, to the three of them sitting up here on what Sandra had thought of up until now as she and Chad's perfectly ordinary conjugal bed.

Now, however, the whole room seemed strange, though not in an unpleasant way. Chad and Desiree, lounging beside her on the bed, were murmuring saucily to each other, and as Sandra watched, she saw Desiree raise her hand and begin to softly stroke Chad's thigh. The younger woman, sensing Sandra's attention on her, glanced up, sending delicious tingling feelings shooting through

Sandra's body as she looked into Desiree's bright, sea-blue eyes.

Then Desiree bit her lip, looking down shyly. The force of her magnetism on Sandra at this moment was such that the older woman began leaning forwards, as though being physically pulled by Desiree's gaze. When Desiree glanced up again Sandra found herself reaching out to her without thinking; and Desiree, smiling sweetly, took Sandra's hand and, looking steadily into her eyes, brought it to her lips.

Sandra sighed profoundly at the touch of her soft mouth, closing her eyes to relish the sensation. When she opened them again, she noticed that Desiree was still stroking Chad's thigh on the other side of her, as she moved Sandra's hand away from her mouth and reached down to her skirt, her hand gliding slowly up to connect with Sandra's bare legs under the thin blue fabric.

Sandra felt her whole body trembling at the touch on her skin, as with a gushing force all of the insanely illicit attraction she had felt for the beautiful woman in the elevator came back to her; yet even more potent here as she stared appreciatively at Desiree's pert and toned body under her tight-fitting clothes. She sighed again, unconsciously moving her legs apart as the other woman's hand moved further up her thigh, gently stroking her in a way in which no female had ever touched her before. Looking up, Sandra saw that Chad was gazing at her with more lust than she had seen on his face for years. Gasping, she caught his eye, licking her lips involuntarily and causing Chad too to sigh in pleasure.

For some moments, then, man and wife looked at each other, lost in the familiarity of each other's eyes contrasted with the bizarreness of the beautiful stranger reclining between them on the bed. It was all so magical, almost too good to be true...

Suddenly the absolute oddness of the situation hit Sandra with full force, like a cold thwack on the head. What on earth were they doing with this girl? Surely it wasn't right? If it was really true that they needed other people in order to make their sex lives happy, wouldn't it be better to simply break up and go their separate ways?

She sat up, shifting uncomfortably; though she had to admit that the touch of Desiree's caress on her skin was feeling better than ever. Chad, sensing Sandra's discomfort, also sat up, and as she caught his eye again, she bit her lip, seeing the doubt which had entered his expression as well.

"We must be crazy," she murmured.

Desiree, catching the sudden change in mood, ceased her stroking, though she did not move her hands away from the couples' legs.

"You guys ok?" she asked softly, looking sidelong at each of them in turn.

Chad licked his lips, which had abruptly gone dry.

"Sandy's right, this is crazy," he said, moving his leg slightly in an attempt to politely extract himself from Desiree's hand.

In the process, however, he moved his crotch closer to her, and she, responding with a fluid motion, which fit his desires so exactly as to seem as though she could hear his thoughts, began dancing her fingers up the center of his groin, smiling as she felt him growing beneath his pants.

"Maybe we should stop this," he gasped, unconvincingly.

Desiree, still flicking her fingers gently all over his now fully erect penis, looked up at him with wide, innocent eyes.

"Stop? Why?" she asked.

Chad groaned.

"Because this is crazy," he said, and Sandra nodded.

There was a pause as Desiree looked from one to the other, eyes still so innocent and blue that both Chad and Sandra felt themselves relaxing a little.

"Well, maybe what we're doing is a little crazy," she agreed, pouting slightly,

"But don't you think..."

Here, she dropped her voice, causing Chad and Sandra to lean forwards, enthralled by her presence as she continued in a sultry whisper,

"Sometimes the best things in life are those which other people call crazy?"

Their faces were very close together now; almost touching; and husband and wife looked at each other, each seeing a new fire slowly lighting in the other's eyes.

"Besides," added Desiree, still whispering seductively,

"I only ever do things if they feel totally right. Are you guys telling me this doesn't feel right?"

Sandra looked down, to see that Chad had reached across to squeeze her reassuringly on the thigh. Something about the way he touched her seemed more fluid than she could ever recall; as though together they were melting in a delicious pool of desire...

"Yes, it feels right," she admitted, Chad nodding firmly as well.

Desiree, looking at both, smiled in an oddly mischievous satisfying way. Neither Sandra nor Chad noticed the impishness of her grin, however; but simply felt themselves pulled forward even more as Desiree murmured,

"Then I guess you also agree that it feels right to do this..."

Gently, she moved her head towards the others, and

before Chad or Sandra could fully register what was happening all three pairs of lips had connected, and they were tasting each other with soft exploration.

As their mouths joined Chad felt his penis instantly respond with an unprecedented passion. Desiree's tongue tasted so sweet; so strangely fresh; in the back of his mind, he had been half-expecting to fall in love with her completely and forget all about Sandra, but as the three tongues began to mingle together, he realized that the opposite was true.

It had been some time since he and Sandra had kissed so intimately anyway, and he could not remember being particularly bowled over with passion whenever they had. Yet the attention which she was giving him now seemed inspired by the younger woman's tongue winding around hers; the whole effect sending him wild with lust. As he continued exploring the two women's mouths hungrily the sensation of their attention became too much for him to continue joining in and he sat back, gasping, and gazing in awe at the sight before him of his own wife rapturously enjoying a tongue-filled kiss with a young and gorgeous blonde.

Suddenly he gasped as his arousal began increasing even more. Looking down, he saw that Desiree still focused intently on Sandra, had also reached out her hand to Chad's groin and was fondling him energetically, causing his already swollen penis to grow even more in her hand. It was becoming almost painful to keep such an erection inside his pants, and without pausing to think he hurriedly began unbuttoning them, Desiree eagerly grabbing the liberated shaft of his dick as he pulled them away from his legs and moved around, sitting on the armchair facing the bed so that he could get the best view. As he did so Desiree continued groping his penis, causing him to thrill with unstoppable hunger, and before he knew what he was doing he had also ripped off his shirt.

With her other arm, Desiree was drawing Sandra close to her, pressing their chests together as they continued exploring each other's mouths. Sandra could feel the younger woman's breasts, pert and stiff-nippled, rubbing deliciously on her own; she remembered now that even before that strange encounter in the elevator she had often used to fantasize about boobs, and the fact that Desiree's were particularly gorgeous was turning her on immensely. But she had to get closer; the tingling sensations, which Desiree was eliciting throughout her body with every flick of her tongue were becoming more and more powerful, and unthinkingly Sandra reached out, taking the other woman's tight white elasticated top and beginning to tug it away.

They broke apart, gasping for air, and Sandra, noticing that she had actually started to undress Desiree, paused and gave an embarrassed smile. Desiree was as unperturbed as ever, though, and with a mischievous grin she reached out to Sandra, slowly beginning to unbutton her blouse. This meant her taking her hand from Chad, so he, eager for more attention, began taking over; ripping the buttons from Sandra's blouse in a frenzy. As he started pulling the blouse away from her, she looked at him, his horniness igniting deep sensations within her; sensations which she had not realized it was even still possible for her to feel. They locked eyes, and at that moment nothing existed except she and her husband lost in the sublimity of pleasure.

Then he smiled, flicking his eyes to Desiree, and she, understanding his suggestion, turned back to her, tentatively beginning to caress her firm chest. Desiree responded, causing Sandra to gasp in wonder as she began fondling her boobs.

Chad was watching approvingly, and noticing that the women's enjoyment was still being hindered by the presence of their clothes, began peeling away the bras: first Sandra, then Desiree. Now they could concentrate on pleasing each other, and he watched, entranced, as Desiree slowly leaned over, sticking her tongue out and giving Sandra's boobs a long and lingering lick. Sandra closed her eyes, and Chad thought he was going to come right there and then as he gazed at her face; so relaxed and full of delight that she seemed the same Sandra he had married all of those years ago.

Gently, Desiree got one of Sandra's breasts in her mouth, rolling her tongue around it in a way, which took Sandra's breath away; and Chad's too, as his dick instantly responded to the idea of what that tongue could do to him. Sandra moaned, sitting up so that she was kneeling on the bed and opening her legs to Desiree. The other woman moved her head down, dragging her tongue over Sandra's belly, causing her to shiver, glancing up at Sandra with those delightful jewel-like eyes as she came to the waistline of her skirt. Chad, again eager to assist, began pulling the skirt off, gripping Sandra's thighs as he did so and marveling at the vitality there which he had not previously noticed.

Sandra was stroking Desiree, taking her luscious breasts in her hand and squeezing them as her husband slid her skirt away, and Desiree sat up, grabbing the hem of Sandra's underpants and curling her fingers firmly around the fabric.

Sandra could feel herself moistening more and more at every touch, and now she watched, moaning softly, as the other woman began decisively pulling her underpants away from her groin. Desiree looked up, blinking in sweet innocent curiosity which immediately set off goose pimples up and down Sandra's entire body.

Now both Chad and Sandra were almost entirely naked but Desiree still had on her tight-fitting hot pants and Chad, keen to address this imbalance, moved forwards, his whole body aching with yearning as his hand connected with Desiree's body again. Her ass was firm and he could not stop himself from gripping it fiercely as he removed the hot pants, causing Desiree to gasp and flick her eyes to him sultrily as she finished undressing Sandra and began dancing her fingers up the older woman's thighs.

Every part of Sandra was aching now for the touch of this exotic stranger; yet when her fingers actually connected with her clitoris it was even lovelier than she could imagine. Tantalizingly, Desiree began pulsating her fingers all around Sandra's entrance, paying special attention to her clit, which was now swollen and dripping. Sandra moaned, shifting around to spread her legs before Desiree as the other woman's fingers began climbing exquisitely into her quivering pussy.

Having peeled away Desiree's hot pants, Chad moved back to her ass, caressing her and sliding his hands around her lace-enclosed cheeks to the front of her underpants. As he did so he gasped; seeing the delectable ecstasy on his wife's face coincide with the feeling of Desiree, hot and already sticky beneath her pants, under his fingers.

Hungrily, he began rubbing Desiree, slipping his fingers in excitement under the soft black lace. As he did so he felt another touch; Sandra was clutching his hand as she, too, began moving her fingers under Desiree's underpants as she started bucking her pussy up and down on the other woman's fingers.

So enthralled was Chad by this that he sat back in the

armchair, groaning as he watched Sandra plunge her hand into that sweet, inviting pussy. His view of this magnificent scene was being obscured slightly by the underpants, however; and with a growl he leaped forwards, unable to stop himself from tearing the last of Desiree's clothes completely away from her body, revealing her soft ass, creamy against the golden tan of the rest of her body. Now Sandra began exploring further into Desiree, her fingers questing urgently as she watched Desiree's face contort with pleasure. Chad, groaning again, grabbed his dick compulsively, rubbing it, unable to take his eyes from them.

Both women were now writhing together on the bed, moaning as they began fingering each other with frantic abandon. Sandra, staring into Desiree's gorgeous face, started pulsating her fingers wildly, absolutely incensed by the soft yelps of passion Desiree was emitting.

"Oh yes!" cried Desiree,

"More, more, give me more!"

She flung out her toned legs, thrusting her pussy forwards onto Sandra's fingers and she, body thrilling with anticipation, plunged her digits even deeper into the hot, inviting pussy before her; searching eagerly for the sweet center.

Chad leaned back in the armchair, so turned on that he had to start rubbing himself furiously, gasping as Sandra began increasing her speed, vibrating her fingers with ever more vigor inside Desiree. She was still gyrating her hips around Desiree's own fingers but somehow she was getting even more pleasure from the delight she was eliciting, and she did not even notice when Desiree paused in her attention to Sandra's pussy as Sandra found her absolute sweet spot and began stimulating it wildly.

"Oh yes!" Desiree cried, arching her back and screwing herself onto Sandra's fingers;

"Right there, give it to me right there!"

"Oh yes!" Sandra cried in surprised adoration, as she felt the ultimate delight of Desiree's juices beginning to pour out over her fingers and her own pussy to respond in exquisite abandon.

"Yes, yes, yes!"

Desiree began thrashing around, her cries reverberating around the whole room, and Chad, enchanted, began pounding his dick with his hand, his cries mingling with those of the women, as all of his horniness at the amazing situation began gushing out of him in a delicious release.

Sandra's entire body was buzzing, and she lay back, dazed and happy, slowly taking her fingers from Desiree's still-throbbing cunt. Looking over, she felt her breath catch at the sight of Desiree, who seemed in that moment to be literally glowing, totally blissed out on the bed next to her. Glancing around, she broke into a wide, uncontrollable grin as she caught sight of her husband, lounging naked in the armchair, his hand still clasped around his shaft, and staring at the pair on the bed as though he had just glimpsed a sighting of angels.

Sensing her gaze on him, he sat up, beaming back at her in a way, which caused Sandra's heart to begin thumping even more than before.

"Wow," he said simply, licking his lips.

"Yeaahh," came Desiree's voice from behind her, and Sandra turned to see the younger woman staring saucily at the pair of them.

"I'm sorry I – finished so quickly," said Chad, looking down in slight embarrassment.

The two ladies spontaneously moved towards him, both

reaching out to stroke his arms reassuringly. It felt so good to be touching her husband at the same time as he was being caressed by the woman who she had brought to such spectacular orgasm. Indeed, everything was feeling good to Sandra now, and she leaned close to Chad, kissing him on the cheek and murmuring,

"No, no, it's fine..."

"Yeah," agreed Desiree,

"We all managed to enjoy ourselves, right?"

Chad and Sandra caught each other's eye.

"Right," they agreed.

Desiree had to leave, but they arranged for her to come round again at the same time the following week. Both Chad and Sandra secretly dreaded that once all were fully dressed the awkwardness of the situation would suddenly hit them; but on the contrary, they parted as though old and very dear friends.

Once Desiree had left they returned to the bedroom, each still tingling with the fantastic events of the evening. Sandra's head was reeling with things she wanted to say to her husband; things which she had been wanting to say to him for months or even years, but which somehow she had felt prohibited to.

"It's so good to feel so open," she exclaimed, running her hand up and down Chad's arm as they lay together on the bed, the scent of the sweat of their adventures still lingering in their nostrils.

"Mmm," agreed Chad.

"It makes me feel as though we really should be together, in spite of all that's happened," added Sandra sincerely.

Chad was silent, and she bit her lip; was she misinterpreting the situation? What if their erotic explorations had elicited in him the exact opposite feeling?

"Chad?" she asked, trying not to let her voice shake too much,

"What do you think?"

She was answered by a faint snore; filling her with an odd mixture of annoyance and utter relief.

Sandra awoke alone, with the sunlight streaming through the curtains that they had forgotten to close hitting her full in the face and momentarily blinding her. Head spinning, she got out of bed, at first highly confused by her unsteadiness, until she remembered that the previous night she had consumed more alcohol than she normally would in an entire month.

"It was totally worth it, though," she murmured as she pulled on her dressing gown, feeling her still-sticky groin tingling at the mere memory of the previous night's antics.

Though Desiree had induced more satisfaction in her than she could remember achieving in a long, long time, she had awoken with a voracious lust, just as though she had not been stimulated at all. Eager to fulfill such an insistent desire, she skipped downstairs, calling in her most seductive voice,

"Chad...?"

She swung her head around the doorway of the lounge and the study; nobody was there. Disappointed, she entered the kitchen, to find it also empty, though on the table was a covered plate and a note.

She took up the note, reading with some dismay that Chad had gone out for the day. However, she was cheered by the frank tone of his writing, as well as the unusual number of kisses at the end of the note. Lately, their lives had become so routine that notes around the house had deteriorated into nothing more than the information required; with this one, though, she could almost feel Chad's arms around her as he promised to be embracing her again soon.

"Breakfast here for you," he said. "Enjoy, my sweet pumpkin."

She gasped, giggling involuntarily at the use of the nickname he had used with her when they had first begun dating; but which he had lately stopped calling her. It made her feel special again, just as she had whenever she spent time with him in the old days.

The breakfast, thanks to being covered, was still hot, and she devoured it hungrily, grateful for the cooked carbs and proteins soaking up the residue of toxins left over from the booze. Then she took out her laptop, vaguely planning to get on with the two or three client orders she had to do for the coming week. Somehow, though, she ended up getting distracted by a group email discussing an event that some of her friends were going to; the annual 'Lake-Dance'. Sandra had been to it many times before; it was one of the city's biggest festivals, and though she had stopped attending in recent years as she told herself she had more serious things to attend to, she had to admit that the email discussion was re-igniting her interest.

She took a break from the computer to go and fetch a coffee, surprised at the force of her enthusiasm. It was just a load of sailing boats doing fancy things out on the water while everyone watched, after all; and she had previously decided that it was a frivolous event designed just for the people of the town to get dressed up in ridiculously decadent costumes to show off to each other while they ate barbecued fish and the city spent thousands of dollars on fireworks and glitz. She had long ago decided that there were more important things in life, yet today somehow the allure of a good party seemed too much to ignore. Perhaps, after all, it would be a perfect place to continue re-igniting her relationship with Chad; if there was any environment where they could relax, the Lake-Dance was sure to be one.

She was becoming more and more titillated by the idea and returning to the computer screen found that the date of this year's event was that very night. It seemed almost fated, and she decided to call Chad and invite him right there and then.

So excited was she that her eagerness was not even dampened by the fact that Chad's phone was off and he was not answering. She decided to simply keep trying at intervals throughout the day, and went back to her homework, but ended up spending the rest of the day simply pottering around the house, too excited to keep her mind on any one thing for an extended period.

She did not really care about the time flying by, with her work still not being done, nor even the fact that despite her trying him four or five times Chad was still not answering. Her mood was wonderfully flippant and blasé, and she even found herself singing as she wandered around the house, doing odd bits of cleaning here and there or occasionally trying on an old piece of clothing to check if she wanted to wear it that evening.

Just as she had more or less decided on her outfit, her phone startled her by ringing and she picked it up, so sure of who it would be that without even looking at the number she answered with a sultry,

"Yes?"

"Well hello there, you sound more cheerful than you have in ages!"

"Oh!" she cried, momentarily flummoxed, then she glanced at the number on the screen.

"I didn't realize it was you, Lisa!" she exclaimed in embarrassment.

"Not to worry." Her friend tittered over the line, and Sandra found herself relaxing.

Lisa was so laid-back that it was difficult to feel awkward around her anyway, and even though Sandra had not actually spoken to her for almost a year now, she did not feel uncomfortable for long.

To her surprise, the reason Lisa was calling was none other than that evening's event.

"I know you probably aren't going, hon," she said,

"But since I'm going to be driving right by your house I thought I'd come and say hello beforehand, that is, if you're not busy?"

Sandra felt a broad smile creeping across her face.

"Busy? Oh no," she said, knowing that she was surprising her friend with uncharacteristic enthusiasm and loving it,

"There's nothing I'd rather do."

As it turned out, Chad had neither come home nor turned his phone on by the time Lisa arrived, so Sandra ended up going to the lake with her girlfriend instead, leaving a note inviting Chad to join them whenever he arrived back.

Lisa continued to be surprised by Sandra's sudden change of attitude, although she had to admit it was a pleasant surprise.

"You know, Sandra, you seem younger," she commented as they arrived at the shore of the lake and grabbed some drinks from a passing waiter with a tray.

"I feel younger," agreed Sandra, gazing out at the boats

weaving around each other just off the shore, their bright, multi-colored sails glowing in the evening sunlight.

Lisa came to stand beside her, and Sandra sighed involuntarily as her friend's shoulder brushed against her own. It had been so long since she had felt she had enough time to simply come out and relax with friends; what had she been so busy doing? None of it seemed relevant now as she stood basking in the warm touch of Lisa's arm on her skin.

The boats were beginning their dance; twisting in and out of each other at crazily close angles, and both women watched, entranced. The different colored sails and the expert way in which the sailors were moving the vessels made them seem almost like a giant, delicate tropical birds floating on the water, involved in some kind of intricately complicated mating ritual, and the whole effect was highly hypnotic. All along the shoreline, the crowd was generally silenced by the awesome sight; only the cries of the barbecue attendants and the odd murmur of conversation breaking the air of expectant wonder.

Closer and closer the boats came to each other; their sails soaking up the orange rays of the fading sun, gloriously bright patches on the blue ripples of the lake. It was the same blue as Desiree's eyes, Sandra thought dreamily; those eyes which had been looking so intensely into hers the previous night...

She smiled, lost in her fantasies; barely noticing that her gaze had wandered away from the bright, weaving tricks of the crafts on the water and down Lisa's chest, alighting unconsciously on her large, chocolate-colored breasts, which were just visible under the collar-line of her turquoise V-neck shirt. Sandra had always admired Lisa's regal, dark-skinned beauty, and now, fuelled by her memories of last night, she found her admiration turning to specific curiosity as her contemplation wandered down Lisa's slim figure to her pert, round ass, and as she recalled how delicious it had felt to slide her fingers into Desiree's sweet, soft pussy, she could not help but wonder how Lisa's might feel as well...

She was startled abruptly from her fantasies by a huge cheer, and shook her head, bringing her hands up to clap along with the rest of the crowd, although she realized that she hadn't a clue how the show had ended. Lisa was whooping happily next to her, and Sandra looked down, ashamed of the graphic nature of her fantasies. Luckily, her friend did not appear to have noticed anything odd in Sandra's behavior, and they began to wander around together, chatting amiably as they sampled the barbecue and saying hello to various people.

It had been so long since Sandra had attended this event that she had forgotten how many people she knew would be there. Normally she disliked being on such a public show; she was always afraid that she would do something weird and the next minute the whole town would know about it. Tonight, though, she felt strangely confident; no doubt aided by Lisa's effervescently sociable nature and greeted all of their acquaintances with a genuine warmth, which quite took her aback.

After a couple of hours of this, however, she began to grow tired. The cumulative effect of last night's drinks and the free wine which was being paraded liberally around the lake shore was taking its toll, and she had to excuse herself to Lisa.

"You're not going to stay for the fireworks?" asked her friend, surprised.

For a second, Sandra was tempted; but she had not been

this sociable for many months and had forgotten how tiring simply hanging out with people could be.

"I can't, I'm falling asleep on my feet," she protested,

"It was really great to see you though."

"You too, hon," replied Lisa warmly, spreading her arms wide to hug.

"Don't leave it so long next time!" she said softly as the women embraced.

"I won't," replied Sandra, trying very hard to be friendly and keep things simple, even though the pressure of Lisa's breasts and the exotic scent of her perfumed skin was setting off all kinds of strange feelings inside her.

She returned home in a pensive mood, to find Chad already asleep. Anyway, she was too sleepy now to play.

As she closed her eyes, myriad images swarmed before them; the strange girl in the elevator, Desiree's mouth on her breasts, Lisa's body pressing against hers. It was strange how turned-on she had been by Lisa tonight. She supposed all of it was a little strange, but then she was too tired to care. The images were pleasant ones, and she drifted off again into salacious dreams filled with half-met desires and alluring temptations.

Over the next few days, it began becoming abundantly clear that the Jones' lives were changing. Although they still had not spent that much time together since that glorious night, whenever they did see each other their exchanges were filled with warm energy rather than crackling tension. Even the reasons why they were not spending so much time together were changing.

The day after the Lake Dance, Sandra was describing how amazing the show had been (what she had been paying attention to, anyway), and how he should have been there when Chad totally surprised her by saying he had been out all day painting. Some years ago, he had told her that he had given up this pastime as he no longer felt inspired, so she was highly eager to see what he had done.

"No way," said Chad, smiling mysteriously,

"It's not ready yet."

So full of creative vitality did he sound that she felt a thrill pass through her whole body at his words. And indeed, she seemed also to be finding the time and inclination to do things, which she previously had thought had gone out of her life forever. One night she got the sudden urge to bake a Banoffee pie; the next, to stay up late designing what to do in their garden. Chad seemed as happy as she with these new activities; it sure made a change from zoning out in front of the TV.

Her colleagues began commenting that Sandra appeared more relaxed, and tasks, which she had used to find a drag suddenly seemed ridiculously easy. Her boss, noticing this improvement in attitude, began entrusting Sandra with more responsibility, something which she had never felt equipped to take on before. Now, however, she found herself accepting it with gusto; so when her boss asked her to attend a conference the next evening in a neighboring state, Sandra said yes immediately.

It meant going out of town and staying in a hotel for a night, so she would spend yet another night without having a proper talk with Chad like she had been hoping to ever since their romp with Desiree. Somehow, though, the talking seemed less important now that the general atmosphere in the house was so much more bearable.

So, she kissed Chad goodbye with more than usual tenderness on the morning of the trip and left him with the house to himself for that evening.

When Chad first arrived home from work he walked around the house, surprised at its emptiness until he remembered where Sandra had gone. Once he did, his first feeling was one of elation that he had the house to himself; but this was immediately tempered by a powerful yearning for his wife as he realized with surprise that the only reason he had longed to be alone there before was that he had not been getting on with Sandra; but now that he was, he really needed her.

It was a hot evening; the hottest of the year so far, his colleagues had informed him. Chad kicked off his shoes and wandered into the lounge, flopping down, hot and sweaty, onto the couch.

"Damn, I wish Sandra was here," he muttered, as he loosened his tie.

Somehow merely the fact that she was not available was making him desperately horny, and he was pretty tempted to simply get his cock out right there and then and satisfy his lust. But he knew it would be nowhere near as pleasing as it would to slip right inside Sandra; slip right up into her hot, wet pussy; so he contented himself with fantasizing about what he was going to do her the following night, and giggling to himself occasionally about how much sexual energy he would have stored up by the time he actually saw Sandra again.

"I won't be able to keep my hands off her," he murmured happily,

"I'll just have to tear her clothes right –"

He was interrupted then, by the loud and sustained ring of the doorbell. So startled was he by the intrusion that he leaped up, hurrying to answer it and completely forgetting the compromising erection showing clearly through his trousers.

"Well *hello*," said the person on the doorstep, and he felt his mouth open in astonishment.

Standing there, dressed in a tight, strapless pink dress, which came down only just over her ripe ass, was Desiree; and although he had not noticed how obvious his horniness was, she certainly had, and was fixing him with a look of lascivious invitation.

"Desiree!" he cried, in utter bewilderment,

"I – what are you doing here?"

"Huh?" she asked, suddenly equally bewildered,

"Didn't you and Sandra invite me here?"

"Oh no," he said, moving inside and frantically searching through the calendar which hung in the hall. "Was that tonight?"

"I certainly thought so," she replied, poking her head around the door to peer at him.

He glanced at her, noticing again how full and round her lips were, and felt his already stiff penis responding as his thoughts wandered involuntarily to what they might feel like wrapped around it.

"Ohhh," he groaned, and then, partly to try to hide his lust, added quickly,

"I'm so sorry! It was supposed to be Friday."

"Oh really?" asked Desiree,

"Ah, no, that's such a shame!"

"It is," agreed Chad, in genuine sorrow.

"I really need to get myself a diary – can't rely on memory all the time!" laughed Desiree.

Chad was pleased to see that she did not seem too annoyed that she had come there for nothing.

"Oh well, I guess I'll leave you in peace then," she said lightly, turning to go.

As she did so her long, golden locks flicked around her

head, sending the aroma of her skin wafting up to tease Chad's nose for just a moment.

He glanced at her, absolute longing throbbing through his every vein. He told himself that it was not longing, however, but merely politeness, which made him say,

"Won't you come in for a coffee anyway?"

Desiree turned back, her bright, sky-blue eyes lighting up merrily.

"You sure you're not too busy?"

"Who's ever too busy to have coffee with a friend?" he replied, holding the door open for her.

"Good answer." She laughed, skipping lightly inside.

Her movements were so graceful that he felt absolutely bewitched by her as he walked behind her swaying ass, following her down the hall. At the stairs, she suddenly paused, laughing lightly as she turned to him with a smile.

"Sorry, I was just heading automatically for the bedroom," she said,

"It's the only place I know! You'll have to show me the kitchen yourself."

"Right!" he replied; for some reason, his voice coming out in a hoarse whisper.

The hallway was quite narrow, and as moved to pass Desiree he had to squeeze his body against hers. He had forgotten again (or had told himself that he had forgotten) about his continuing erection until it was actually rubbing on her crotch, and by then it was too late. He tried to force himself to think of cold showers and trips to the mountains, but her sweet gaze was on him, and try as he may, his mind was filled instead with nothing but her warm flesh.

"Uh, sorry," he muttered, meaning to move swiftly past Desiree towards the kitchen, but somehow finding himself locked into her blue gaze.

"No problem," she said, also unaccountably whispering, "It's nothing we haven't done before..."

"No, I – I guess not," he said, swallowing.

He could sense where this was leading; or at least, where he desperately wanted it to lead. Yet his relationship with Sandra had, over the last few days, improved so dramatically that he was loathed to do anything to upset the balance now. And he was pretty sure that engaging in erotic relationships without Sandra was not likely to help their situation.

It sure felt good as he moved past Desiree, though; his erection slipping on the material of her dress.

Then he was in front of her and the spell was broken; moving purposefully, he entered the kitchen and began clattering around finding the coffee things.

"It's a really nice place you've got here," said Desiree approvingly, sliding onto one of the chairs with that incredible grace, which seemed to come so naturally to her.

"Yes, well, it's not too bad, I suppose," said Chad distractedly, though in truth he had not registered a word of what she was saying.

Concentrate on the coffee; just concentrate on the coffee and it'll all be fine, he thought, struggling manfully to keep his eyes on the task in hand and away from the luscious vision before him.

Desiree was continuing to chatter good-naturedly, putting him more at ease, and he managed to provide what he hoped were convincing answers to most of her questions as he focused on making their beverages. So intent was he on this that he failed to notice Desiree's mischievous grins as she flicked her gaze over him, or her surreptitious glances around the room as she took it all in.

Finally, after what seemed like an absurdly long time,

he set the steaming mugs on the table and sank into the chair beside Desiree. She took her mug, slurping from it happily in a way, which instantly made Chad's knees go weak.

"It's delicious," she said,

"Thanks."

"Yes, it's good quality coffee," he agreed, picking up his own and taking a sip; though his mind was far from the drink.

"I always say I'm gonna go without coffee for a week or so, but I never quite make it," she commented,

"I guess it's one of my guilty pleasures..."

"Oh, is it?" he asked, breathlessly,

"Yes, I know what you mean, no matter how often I say I'm going to quit, there's just something so good about it which means I keep going back..."

"Maybe when something feels so good we shouldn't be fighting our desire for it," pointed out Desiree, her eyes flashing at him in unmistakable invitation.

There was silence for a beat or two, as they sat, eyes locked on each other. Then, before Chad was barely aware of what was happening, they had pounced on each other, and Chad was revolving his hips around against Desiree's as their lips locked together.

Her tongue was soft and tasted so good that he began moaning into her mouth as he curled his around it; and he clutched her to him, drinking in her sweetness, a great urge to devour her right there and then filling him so potently he was not sure where to begin.

Desiree seemed equally incensed; she began tugging frantically at Chad's shirt, ripping one of the buttons completely away in her haste to remove it from his torso. He was already sweating with desire and anticipation, and as he pressed her to him she began rubbing her chest on his, sliding delightfully on his slippery skin. His hands were wandering all over her body; her ass; her back; her bare thighs under the tight, short dress; and now he found the halter neck strap attaching it to her body and furiously began tugging it loose.

Desiree moaned softly as he flung the strap back, peeling the tight pink fabric away from her chest to reveal her pert, golden boobs. Unable to resist them, he plunged his head into her cleavage, nibbling and licking her and uttering soft moans of utter delight at the gorgeousness of her breasts. So excited was he that in doing this he managed to push her back into her chair, and as she sat, wriggling her shoulders delightedly to Chad's attention, she reached for his pants, removing them with a swiftness which under any other circumstances Chad may have found slightly suspicious. Right now he had no thoughts for anything save the taste of Desiree's skin, though; and now he began moaning louder as he felt her delicate hand dancing all around his balls, fondling them delectably, and then skipping lightly up his by now heavily engorged shaft.

So amazing did her hand feel that Chad straightened, standing up before her and thrusting his dick forwards for her to caress more. Seeing this as an invitation, she licked her full, pink lips; just this act alone enough to make Chad shudder in anticipation, and then slowly moved her head down to take the tip of his penis in her mouth.

"Oh wow yeah," he groaned, sliding himself forward, unable to stop, and she took him eagerly right inside her mouth, sliding her lips around him as she began sucking him with tender enthusiasm.

Her mouth was so incredibly hot, and her tongue was flicking so deliciously all around his dick, that he felt almost ready to come right there and then. Incredible fizzing sensations were building up all through his body, and he clutched Desiree's long blonde mane, gasping as she began sucking even harder, slurping on his dick hungrily as she began pumping her mouth up and down in a hypnotic rhythm.

"Oh yeah, just like that; just like that!" he cried, his whole being ready to explode in a massive force of pleasure.

At that moment, however, instead of continuing her sucking, Desiree took him out of her mouth completely, and sat up, gazing at him with the naughtiest smile he had yet seen.

"What do you say we take this... upstairs?" she asked.

He felt right then that if she had suggested going to the ends of the earth he would have agreed. Dumbly, he followed her as she led the way to the bedroom, clawing at the dress which still hung about her midriff so that she could step out of it as she walked along.

As soon as they were in the bedroom, she flung herself on the bed, fixing him with a steady gaze as she asked,

"Do you know how much you're turning me on?"

"Oh god..." breathed Chad, approaching her excitedly as she began wriggling out of her underpants.

"I think you need to give me what I need," she whispered, and he came to her instantly, taking his dick in his hand and moaning as she rolled onto her back, spreading her legs wide to invite him in.

Now that he was actually about to put his dick inside someone other than Sandra he felt suddenly wary. Was this really a good idea?

Desiree answered his question by bucking her pussy up so that her sticky clitoris began rubbing alluringly all around the head of his dick. He shivered, moving inexorably closer to her.

"Feel good?" she asked, looking at him saucily.

"Uh-huh," he replied, barely thinking as he slid his penis fully inside her, making her moan happily.

"Then let's keep doing it," she murmured.

He did not need any encouragement. The words were not even out of her mouth when he began thrusting himself in and out of her, gasping at the fantastic feeling of her tight, wet pussy squeezing him in warm welcome. Desiree began gyrating her hips around, pulling him even deeper inside her, and he groaned, suddenly unable to keep any semblance of control about himself. He simply wanted this woman too badly; he had to have her, and now.

With a growl, he grabbed Desiree's ass, pulling her forwards onto him as he began pounding her, pumping his dick in and out of her with more energy than he knew he possessed.

"Oh yes! That's it!" cried Desiree, and he growled again, clutching her ecstatically as they began fucking with animalistic abandon, and he felt the huge wave, now ten times stronger than before, building up inside him to an incredible peak.

"Oh yeah!" he cried, his entire body pulsating wildly as he plunged into her, pouring his orgasm deep inside her.

She was crying out too; squeezing him so delightfully with her pussy that she prolonged his orgasm, as they lay writhing and shouting together, lost in the sublime sensations of their attraction.

This has to be worth it, Chad thought, when he could think again,

'Just as long as Sandra never finds out...'

Sandra's thoughts at that moment were in fact very far away from her husband. The hotel staff had gotten her boss's order confused, and instead of staying in a single room, she had ended up having to share with a stranger. At first, Sandra was a little put out by this, but as she entered the room, not thinking to knock, she was greeted by an arresting sight.

Standing before her, and for some reason not in the least bit embarrassed, was a beautiful and entirely naked woman.

"Oh, I'm sorry!" she said, laughing,

"I just got out of the shower. Are you here for the conference?"

"Y-yes," Sandra managed to stammer, trying to keep the deep lust, which had begun throbbing through her from her voice,

"I'm sharing a room with you."

"I gathered!" replied the stranger, laughing again,

"To be honest, I'm quite glad. These business trips can get so lonely, you know? It's always good to have some company...oh, do excuse me, there I go, prattling away when you haven't even come in yet!"

She stood aside, and Sandra walked swiftly into the room, trying not to stare too obviously at the stranger's magnificent porcelain skin.

"Anyway, like I was saying," the woman continued, completely unperturbed,

"I always prefer to have a little company, you know, for going to dinner and stuff. That is if you think you'd like to join me?"

Something was making Sandra unable to speak properly at this point; all she could do was nod fervently in affirmation.

CHAPTER 3

DESIRE REAWAKENED: THE THRILL OF THE GAME BOOK 3

THE HOTEL DINING hall was busy, the murmur of the guests thankfully drowning out the sickly blare of the bland 'music' emanating from the speakers. As in most of the faux-classy hotels Sandra had been to on business trips before, there was something about the entire decor, which made one very slightly, but very definitely, ill at ease. Perhaps it was that the glare of the lights was just a shade too bright, or the patterns on the carpet a tiny bit too blobby. Whatever it was, Sandra did not waste too much thought on it. The woman sitting opposite her was far too interesting to get distracted by such matters, and she leaned forwards, intent on the story which Lily - for that was her table companion's name - was in the middle of telling.

"And then what did you do?" she asked, shocked.

"Well, at first I wasn't sure at all whether or not to keep going through with it," Lily replied,

"But then I realized..."

Here she also leaned forwards, so that her milk-white face was just a couple of inches from Sandra's,

"Well, hey, if I don't stand up for what I deserve, then who is going to?"

"And did he agree?"

Lily sat back, nodding serenely, and Sandra did as well, digesting this with some awe.

"I don't think I'd ever have the confidence to do that," she admitted, but Lily waved her hand dismissively at this.

"It's not really about having confidence," she said, picking up her fork and resuming her meal.

Sandra looked down, realizing that she had been so taken in by Lily's story that she had forgotten all about her food as well. Indeed, it was not just the words of the woman before her, which were captivating her; but everything about her manner- her easy grace, her quiet self-assurance, and not least of all her stunning beauty. This latter Sandra was trying very determinedly to forget about. Something about Lily's long, elegant body, her pale, unblemished skin and the contrast of her deep, chestnut hair with her sparkling green eyes was attracting Sandra incredibly, and even here in the crowded dining hall, she could not stop her pussy from tingling in heady longing at the sight of this gorgeous vision.

She shook her head, concentrating very hard on her pasta as she told herself off. What was wrong with her, that she was having such inappropriate feelings? She'd only just met this woman, after all.

You hadn't met Desiree more than a few hours before you were making her come all over your hand, came the unbidden thought in her head, and she bit her lip, hoping against hope that Lily was unable to detect the inner turmoil she was contending with.

"What did you say?" she asked, in an effort to distract

herself from these thoughts, and Lily leaned forwards again, repeating,

"I said, it's about being sure that what you are doing is right."

Sandra looked up, meeting Lily's verdant eyes and staring into them, momentarily lost for what to say. Her pussy had instantly responded to Lily's words; so close were they to what Desiree had been saying to her on that mind-blowing night last week. As she gazed at Lily, she could not help a twinge of hope flicker within her. Could it be possible that Lily was feeling the same way as she?

But the other woman had turned back to her food again, and Sandra was about to also continue eating when her eyes inadvertently started wandering over her companion's chest. With a sharp thrill, she realized that below the sheer, delicate fabric of Lily's dress she was not wearing any bra; and as Sandra gazed at her, she could clearly make out the pert nipples showing through. Just then Lily glanced up and Sandra hurriedly flicked her eyes back to her plate, managing as she did so to just about muster some self-control over her emotions.

Luckily, Lily soon began chatting again, seemingly not aware of the struggle Sandra was enduring to hide her attraction to her, and in truth, her conversation did succeed in arresting Sandra's attention again, for she seemed to have been involved in a huge variety of fascinating things, and she was a good story-teller. Throughout the evening, Sandra listened in amusement to her tales of life modeling, visiting erotic dance clubs to find out the girls' working conditions and being chased away by the manager, getting caught in the rain before a big important presentation to clients, and passing off her wet attire as an illustration of the presentation theme.

What Sandra was enjoying, even more, was not Lily's ability to speak, but her willingness to listen. She often asked Sandra questions and would gaze in rapt attention at her as Sandra went over her feelings. When Sandra told Lily about the Lake Dance which she had attended the other day, her whole face lit up with a radiance so lovely Sandra felt for a split second that she would explode with longing right there and then.

"Sounds amazing! And did you go out on the lake?" asked Lily eagerly, dragging Sandra back to the present.

"Well, not this year," she said,

"But I did go one time in one of the dancing boats."

It had been years ago before she had met Chad even, and this evening was the first time she had recalled it for many years. Lily was gazing at her expectantly and so she felt compelled to dig deeper into her memory, feeling the wind rushing past her face once more and the thrill of the other boats, sails glowing in the afternoon sun, whizzing past hers and just missing it.

"It was incredible," she said dreamily, and Lily nodded, absorbing her delight.

"I adore being out on the water," she commented,

"It feels so - liberating..."

"Yes," agreed Sandra,

"I'd like to do it more..."

She looked up, meeting Lily's eyes again and seeing in them this time a definite mischievous gleam. But what could it mean?

Then the spell was broken and the other woman had turned back to her salad.

"You tempted by the idea of checking out the nightlife of this town?" she asked casually, causing Sandra to frown in consternation.

Normally this idea would be automatically off-putting to her, but she was desperate to spend as much time as possible with this fantastic lady, so she said noncommittally,

"Um, I don't know what kind of nightlife there is here, I've never been here before. What do you think?"

Lily shrugged, spearing a piece of tomato with some gusto.

"I'm pretty tired," she said,

"Might just head up to my room. Sorry - our room," she added, smiling cheekily at Sandra.

"Oh, I'm very happy to just relax as well," she agreed, hoping she did not sound too clingy.

"Cool," replied the other simply, and Sandra felt her shoulders drop at the release of a tension she had not even realized she was holding there.

"Cool," she agreed.

━━

Try as she might to act as though everything was perfectly normal, Sandra could not help feeling distinctly nervous as they made their way to the room, and so resigned was she to the fact that however much Lily might get on with her, there was no sexual attraction there, that she considered simply going straight to sleep to avoid too much rejection. Almost as soon as they were in the room, however, Lily, after rooting around in her suitcase, suddenly produced a bottle of wine and held it up to Sandra with a naughty smile.

"I know it's probably not a good idea the night before we have to speak in front of a bunch of people," she said,

"But it might be nice..."

Her smile turned Sandra on more than she could

possibly comprehend, and her mind had already begun racing as far as how she could turn the drinking, somehow, to a more intimate encounter. Then she scolded herself, realizing that however much she may want to if she did end up actually manipulating the situation she would definitely regret it.

I've made a lovely friend tonight; can't I be content with that? she thought impatiently, though her pussy was aching to disagree.

Lily poured the wine and they clinked glasses, sipping slowly. Any kind of awkward atmosphere which may have ensued from Sandra's inner tension was swiftly dispelled by Lily's easy chatter, and Sandra found herself relaxing in spite of herself as they sat together on Lily's bed, since that was the one against the wall, which they could lean on.

"Normally these conferences are so dull," Lily commented,

"Sometimes I try and slip some subtle jokes into my presentation, just to liven the place up."

"Wow, I never thought to do that," replied Sandra, biting her lip as she thought about what she had to say the following day.

It was merely an introduction of her company, something which, as someone who had been working there for six years, she had felt pretty well equipped now. But what if the audience got bored?

So distracted was she by these worries that she missed the next thing the other woman said.

"Huh?" she asked.

"I said, I'm really glad I found you here tonight," smiled Lily,

"You've really made staying here a whole lot nicer."

She beamed at Sandra, whose thoughts were still half on her presentation, so she merely nodded absently.

Lily suddenly burst into laughter: startling Sandra with its wild peals.

"You know, you gave me such a shock when you first came in here!" she cried,

"Do you remember?"

"Did I?" Sandra asked, casting her mind back in fondness to the glorious scene which had greeted her when she first entered the hotel room earlier that evening.

Lily nodded, still giggling, and looking at Sandra sidelong in a strangely penetrating fashion which Sandra did not notice.

"Caught me completely by surprise!" she added.

"Wow, you didn't show it," pointed out Sandra,

"I was really impressed by your confidence at being naked in front of a complete stranger!"

"Were you?" inquired Lily with deep interest,

"Well, that calls for more drink!"

She filled up their glasses, and Sandra took hers, suddenly noticing the deep mischievous gleam in Lily's eyes.

"So you weren't really just comfortable standing there?" she asked, gazing at her admiringly, and Lily shook her head.

"You just came in on me so suddenly, I didn't know what to do!" she explained. "So I thought the best thing would be to just act normal and pretend this was exactly what I was planning..."

Both women burst into laughter at this, and Sandra drank some more wine, a mixture of admiration and relief filling her. So Lily was not simply some kind of super-confident woman; she could get uncomfortable too.

"I have to say, that is the only time you've made me uncomfortable since I met you," Lily went on. "In fact, even when you first walked in, I was only uncomfortable for a second or two. I could just feel there's something about you which I knew instantly I liked - I'm generally right about these things..."

She put down her glass, shifting a tiny bit closer to Sandra on the bed, and Sandra jumped slightly as she reached out, taking a lock of her brown hair and pushing it gently behind her ears.

"It was annoying me," explained Lily. "I couldn't see your face properly."

"Your hands are so soft!" commented Sandra before she had time to think of what she was saying.

Lily brought her hand up again, this time running the back of it over Sandra's cheek, and try as she might to keep some kind of self-control, the latter could not help sighing yearningly.

"Sandra," Lily said gently. "I know this might sound crazy, but - well, I just get such a strong feeling about this. And like I say, I'm generally right in my feelings..."

She had not stopped stroking her face, and Sandra sat very still, hardly daring to breathe now, lest she breaks the wonderful magic which seemed suddenly to be happening.

"And I'm not really one for exploring too much, especially with someone I've just met," added Lily. "But with you, it just feels so right that we do so..."

Sandra licked her lips, which had unaccountably gone dry. "What do you want to explore?" she asked, heart pounding at what she hoped would be the answer.

"You," was the unambiguous reply, and barely had Lily

finished saying it than she had glided over to Sandra, moving her face to hers and kissing her in a soft, fluid motion which made Sandra unsure whether or not she was dreaming.

Lily's lips were even suppler than they looked, and Sandra opened her mouth, moaning slightly as Lily slowly slid her tongue out and began revolving it all around hers. The sensation was deliciously heady, and Sandra felt almost as though they were melting together. Barely aware of what she was doing, she clutched Lily, doing what she had been longing to do all night and pulling her slim, elegant body to her own as they continued kissing with breathtaking tenderness.

Lily moved her hand down Sandra's cheek, massaging her shoulder and moving down her body, to rest on her thigh, squeezing it provocatively. Sandra was almost too shocked to take this in; it all seemed too perfect, too, in line with the illicit fantasies she had been desperately trying to get rid of all night, and she broke her face apart from the other woman's, gazing at her in incredulity.

"I've been wanting to do that all night," said the other, eyes flashing deliciously at her.

"You – you have?" gasped Sandra.

"You're just such a gorgeous woman, Sandra, I – I couldn't help feeling incredibly attracted to you," affirmed Lily, gripping her thigh once more.

"Oh really?" Sandra breathed, moving closer to her and wriggling her groin almost unconsciously in response to Lily's attention,

"And do you still feel like that?"

"Very much so," replied the other woman, suddenly sitting up straight and looking her right in the eye,

"What do you think we should do about it?"

For a heartbeat, then, the two were still, eyes locked together. Then the build-up of the intense chemistry of the evening took over, and they pounced, each barely aware of what was happening as they embraced roughly, lying back and rolling together on the bed as they began kissing again, more passionately this time, with fierce desire.

Lily's hands were moving under Sandra's skirt, setting her aflame with lust, and she reciprocated eagerly, finding the silken hem of the thin fabric of Lily's dress and pulling it up inquisitively. Lily sighed, gyrating her hips against Sandra's and causing her to begin moistening unstoppably as she continued tugging at Lily's dress and the latter compliantly disentangled her arms from their embrace, holding them above her head so Sandra could pull the dress off her completely.

Everything was going so deliciously in accord with her fantasies that Sandra was beyond incredulity by now, and simply accepted that she now had Lily's near-naked body in her arms as a matter of course. Lily was sighing in an absolutely heavenly manner as Sandra began caressing her smooth, pale skin, marveling at the softness and the radiance of her body which almost made it seem as though she was glowing palely under Sandra's darker, tanned hands.

"Mmm," murmured Lily, writhing delightfully. "That feels amazing..."

Reaching out, she grabbed Sandra's skirt again, sliding her hands underneath it, and Sandra gasped as her slender fingers began connecting with her already-sodden underwear. Moaning, Sandra began bucking her pussy against Lily's hand, so turned on by now that even through her clothes the other woman's touch was sending her wild with the titillation.

Smiling naughtily, Lily curled her fingers around the

waistband of Sandra's underpants, finding her sticky clitoris and revolving her hand around it, causing Sandra to shudder and moan.

"Oh wow, Sandra," she said. "You turn me on so much..."

"You do the same," gasped Sandra, running her hands down Lily's creamy back, grabbing her thin lace underpants and pulling them swiftly away.

Lily moved closer to her, hooking one leg over Sandra's body as she did the same ejection of Sandra's underpants, and began undulating her naked body against Sandra, causing her to cry out in adoration at the fantastic fizzing sensations being elicited throughout her body. Hungrily, she reached for Lily, gripping her small, round ass cheek with one hand and moving the other steadily over her slim, dainty stomach to the dark triangle of her pubic hair.

As her fingers connected with it, she moaned again, feeling the delicious slipperiness of Lily's juices. The other woman was gazing at her expectantly, still dancing her fingers all around Sandra's clitoris in exquisite effusiveness, and Sandra, crying in excitement, plunged her hand inside the dark, inviting triangle, finding the slick sensitive nub therein and vibrating her hand all around it.

"Oh God, yeah," moaned Lily, thrusting her pussy forwards and backward, playing with herself delectably on Sandra's fingers, and the latter stared, almost too stunned by the devastating beauty of this incredible woman to move, face contorting in unselfconscious delight as Sandra began exploring deeper inside her, watching her gorgeous expressions to see where she was stimulating her the most.

Lily responded by pushing her fingers further inside Sandra too, and she gasped, spreading her legs wide and squeezing her, inviting her to come right up inside her. She eagerly fingered Lily with mounting vigor now, and she started humping her fingers uncontrollably as Lily, questing ever deeper, began flicking her hand all around inside Sandra, thrilling her with dizzying new sensations.

Every move, which this exquisite lady made inside her, seemed to be finding all of the exact spots which needed stimulation, and Sandra squirmed, jerking her hips more and more, as she felt Lily begin connecting with all of the sweet spots of her being; enticing her to open up to the intense throbbing blaze of pleasure which was building up inexorably all around her now.

Incensed, she began waggling her fingers frenetically inside Lily, smiling as she felt her too beginning to open, and suddenly sensing the wave of pleasure rising to full force, she started increasing the tempo, even more, howling in ecstasy as Lily found her innermost core and began opening her up, so that her juices started gushing intensely all over the slender hands.

Lily, also screaming in delight, gripped Sandra hard, pumping her pussy manically on her fingers so that she also began flowing with sweet, ecstatic syrup, her face twisting in such profound rapture that she prolonged Sandra's own orgasm for some time as they lay, writhing together, sticky and blissful.

Sandra still had not stopped thinking about Lily by the time she returned to her hometown; her entire being was buzzing with the glorious satisfaction of their activities. She was a little confused, however, by what she was going to say to Chad. Part of her simply wanted to introduce Lily into their marital love-making as soon as possible; she was sure Chad would enjoy it, and the idea was intensely thrilling. She did not feel in the least bit guilty for sleeping with someone away from Chad; what she had shared with Lily felt somehow too pure and right for her to even consider that she had done something bad. Yet this did not stop the fact that try as she may to find an appropriate way to tell her husband what she had been up to, she could not settle on one which would not make him angry, or at the very least wildly suspicious.

When she got to their house, it was already dark, and she could see that Chad was in. As the time for actually facing him drew closer she realized with certainty that she was in no way ready to deal with the consequences of admitting her actions, and resolved right there and then to keep them a secret; for now, at least.

It's not like it will be the first secret we've had between us, she thought as she stood on the doorstep, fumbling for her key; after all, over the past couple of years, the couple had had so many communication problems that at times she had felt she had not known him at all.

Even so, when Chad asked her how it had gone at the conference, she could not help flicking her eyes away from his jumpily.

"Oh, fine, fine," she said airily, and then, more to change the subject than anything else, moved forwards, coming to stand before him as he sat at the kitchen table.

"I missed you," she said, and he rose, taking her in a warmer embrace than she had been expecting, considering that her words were not entirely true.

"I missed you too," he murmured, kissing her hair; she was too intent on concealing her own emotions to notice the insincerity of his tone.

Lily's gorgeous emerald eyes were dancing before her vision; her wild, dark hair flinging fantastically behind her head as she lay, screaming with passion-

She dragged herself back to the present, realizing with a

start that Chad was holding her by the shoulders, staring into her eyes with some concern.

"Are you ok?" he asked, stroking her shoulders considerately.

"Mmm," she said absently, and then, seeing how caring he was being, shook herself mentally.

She had to stop thinking of Lily; it was not fair when her husband was standing right here being so kind to her.

"Mmm," she said again, as he started kneading her shoulders, still gazing at her with some anxiety. "That feels nice..."

As she brought her focus fully into the room and away from her flashbacks of the previous night she realized how delicious Chad's warm, firm touch was, and wriggled appreciatively, sighing as he started massaging her even more firmly, with such potent force that he pushed her back onto the table, and she sat on it, kicking her shoes off and wrapping her legs around his torso to pull him to her.

"I really did miss you," she murmured, more as a reassurance to herself than to him, but causing his eyes to light up with desire nevertheless.

"I was fantasizing about you while you were gone," he admitted, moving his hands down her back so that she arched her spine, gasping.

"About doing what?" she asked breathlessly, her body pulsing with electrical tingles as he continued caressing her back with smooth, generous palm strokes.

"Oh, slipping my fingers into some...nice places," he grinned, though at that moment his inner vision was filled with nothing but Desiree's tight, hot cunt as she thrust it in his face, moaning,

"Keep doing that!"

"Mmm," said Sandra again, desire pulsing through her

as she felt his erection swelling and growing beneath his pants, and she reached out, pulling his flies undone and taking it with a firm grip.

Chad groaned, fixing his eyes on hers and shaking himself mentally for getting lost in fantasies about Desiree. This was no time for that; wasn't an erotic romp alone with Sandra just what he had been waiting for?

"Keep doing that," he murmured, concentrating now on Sandra only, as she started sliding her hand enticingly up and down his ever-growing shaft.

Excitedly, he reached around his wife's ass, finding the zip of her skirt and tugging it impatiently down, pawing away the crisp black fabric. Sandra wriggled on his hands, facilitating the undressing process, every move that Chad made now causing her to become wetter and wetter with an insatiability, which she had rarely felt for her husband, even back when they had first started sleeping together. She had to have more of him, and she lunged forwards, taking her underpants with one hand and wriggling out of them, while with the other hand she grabbed his cock firmly and brought it to her entrance, to begin rubbing the head of his dick all around her eager opening. He sighed, jerking his hips appreciatively, and then began moaning as she brought her other hand up to start caressing his balls with touching sweetness.

"Oh yeah, Sandra, that's right..." he moaned, taking her ass cheeks with both hands and thrusting himself forwards on her, and she, smiling mischievously, began guiding his dick, vibrating the sensitive head all around her clitoris so that both began shivering in ecstasy.

Sighing, she flung her legs wide, and he bit his lip, astounded by how horny she was making him. She was rolling her hips all around his dick with provocative grace now; her movements so uncharacteristically erotic that he felt almost as though he was making love to a new woman, and he realized with a mounting passion that he had to explore this new woman more, right now.

Growling, he gripped her harder, sliding up, right up inside her, and her eyes widened as she felt him connecting with all of the yummiest parts of her. Even her pussy felt different today, and as he started moving faster, thrusting his dick in and out of her intently, she opened up even wider, flinging her legs high up behind his back and then, as he responded by plunging even deeper into her, wrapping them around him with a violent force.

He was beginning to penetrate her now with astounding profundity and he laid her down on the table, both unheeding of the rhythmic din as he stood over her, fucking her now with animalistic intensity as she gripped him hard with her creamy thighs, bucking her pussy up and down and crying, delectably,

"More!"

"Damn right I'll give you more!" he snarled, increasing his thrusting with an urgent compulsion as he felt her coming closer and closer to drawing from him his innermost seeds. She was squeezing him so tightly now that it felt almost as good as the way that Desiree squeezed him; at this thought, he began crying out, overwhelmed by sweet pleasure as he started pulsating wildly inside Sandra, spilling himself into her, though forgetting for a moment who she was.

Sandra felt him beginning to climax with heady anticipation and started pounding her pussy up and down furiously, sensing him stimulating her to her very core. He was finding all of her most sensitive places, almost as exquisitely as Lily had done; with this thought, she began screaming,

Chad's orgasm gushing inside her, but her mind firmly on a different person entirely as her climax washed through them.

That evening they slept in each other's arms, each assuring the other that they were intensely satisfied, though each secretly desiring something quite different. As they prepared to leave for work the following morning, they said goodbye amiably enough; but each was busy fantasizing over their recent extra-marital exploits.

Something about the fresh smell of the unusually cool breeze coming in from the lake, relieving some of the oppressive summer heat as Sandra walked down the main street towards work, was causing her heart to lift in excitement. She knew she should not be thinking of Lily, but the freshness of the day seemed to be reminding her of her delightful skin and pleasant aroma, and the thought of her hot, wet pussy throbbing under Sandra's fingers was simply too tantalizing to push away...

Besides, she told herself firmly, why should she stop thinking about Lily, when it clearly felt so right to do so?

Anyway, she was sure that things would become easier with Chad as time went on. After all, the following night was their pre-arranged appointment with Desiree, and Sandra was sure that even if Chad could not completely quell her fantasies over Lily, Desiree and her ripe young body would soon be able to distract her.

Satisfied with these thoughts, Sandra got on with most of the morning's work in relative peace. The equilibrium was disturbed, however, when her phone purred in her pocket and, taking it out, she saw with a thrill that it was a message from Lily.

"I'm in your town tonight. Any chance you want to meet up to play? X."

Just these words alone were enough to make Sandra hot all over, and she glanced around nervously, sighing in relief that none of her colleagues were paying any attention to her.

But I should just ignore it' she thought firmly, turning back to her reports, I have Chad and Desiree, bringing her into it as well would just be too complicated...

Still, the thought would not leave her head, and after some minutes of totally failing to re-focus on her work, she sighed, grabbing her phone and slipping into the office corridor.

"Hello, honey," Chad answered in some surprise. "Aren't you at work?"

"Yeah," she said, trying to make her voice as regretful as possible,

"And they've just given me a lot more reports on clients to do which have to be completed for tomorrow morning. I don't think I'll be home until at least nine."

"Oh no, really?"

She sighed, so dramatically that she even half-convinced herself of the truth of her words. "I'm sorry, darling."

"That's ok, it's not your fault," Chad said reassuringly, momentarily causing a stab of guilt in her stomach. "I have to go out anyway to do this evaluation for Tom."

"Oh!" she said, intrigued, though trying not to show it. "Where are you going?"

"Out to the other side of the lake," he explained. "I probably won't be home before you anyway."

"Oh, ok, then," she said. "Well, at least we will have proper time to play together tomorrow night."

"Mmm hmm," he agreed, though his thoughts were already wandering.

After they hung up, he sat back, body thrilling with the illicit idea which had occurred to him as they had been speaking, and which had caused him to tell his wife that complete fabrication about the work he had to do. It was naughty; of that, he had no doubt. But at the same time, it felt too good to ignore.

Hands shaking with eagerness, he reached for his phone again and pressed Desiree's number with some deliberation.

"So you want me there tonight instead of tomorrow night?" asked Desiree.

I want you here tonight, and every night, you sexy minx, he thought, but out loud, he said. "No no no, I want you to come here both nights. That is if you can..."

"Yes, I think I can make that," she purred. "I'll come both nights... What time?"

"Six," he said; easily enough time to fuck her senseless and for her to leave before Sandra returned, he reasoned.

"See you then," she said saucily.

"I can't wait," he growled and was just about to put the phone down when a thought occurred to him.

"Uh, Desiree, one more thing," he said hurriedly,

"I want you to come in through the back door. You just go round the alleyway to the left of the house and through the little gate."

"Why?" asked Desiree, her voice smoldering with impish curiosity.

"Just... it'll be more fun," he explained. "I'll leave the door open for you. Please come that way."

"Well... ok then," she agreed. "I'll come that way."

He hung up for real then, before she began arousing him too much.

He would just have a quick romp with Desiree tonight; just enough to satisfy this deep, urgent craving she had managed to awaken in him. Sandra never needed to know anything about it; would never be able to find out, in fact, as his clever instructions to Desiree meant that even if any neighbors were to see her, they would not know she was going to his house.

"It'll be good for our marriage in the long run," he said out loud, though he was not sure he was convinced.

At first, Sandra had been planning to meet up with Lily just for drinks in a bar somewhere, but Chad's news had changed things dramatically. If the house was going to be empty for some time that evening it seemed too good an opportunity to miss. She could meet Lily there just long enough for them to fuck each other senselessly and then go out to a bar, leaving Chad none the wiser.

"It must be fate," she decided, eagerly dialing Lily's number.

"I just thought it might be nice for you to come round for a bit, you know, just to... relax," she explained.

"Sounds perfect," Lily purred,

"What time?"

"Uh... six," said Sandra; she wanted them to have as much time as possible, and her office did not close until five-thirty.

"Ok, I'll come at six," agreed Lily.

"Looking forward to it," said Sandra breathlessly, then, just as Lily was about to hang up added, "Wait! I forgot something!"

"What?" asked Lily, her piqued curiosity sending Sandra dizzy with arousal.

"Just, the front door's um... a little broken," she said, improvising desperately; she had just remembered how awkward it might look if any of the neighbors saw Lily going into their house.

"Go round the house to the side and come in through the back door. I'll leave it open for you."

"Sure, no problem," agreed Lily,

"I'll come that way."

"I can't wait," murmured Sandra, then hung up before she became so horny that she would have to go and start touching herself before she felt fit to return to work.

No, she could wait until this evening. Smiling, she returned to her desk, hardly daring to believe that she was actually going to go through with such a clearly compromising meeting.

I'm not betraying him, he just wouldn't understand if I was to tell him, she reasoned to herself, only managing to believe this, however, for a second or two.

The house was dark and calm, the garden mysterious in the long shadows of the evening sunlight, as Lily made her way, heart pumping, through the little gate and towards the kitchen door leading onto the garden patio. Opening it, she saw at once the shape of a woman, and greeted her warmly,

"Well hello there..."

"Hello?" came the surprised reply, and she paused, blinking in the abrupt brightness of the light, which the room's other occupant had just flicked on.

"Oh!" she said with some surprise, as she saw that the woman before her was not Sandra, but someone much younger, her long, flowing blonde hair cascading over her pert breasts, only just held in by the tight red halter-neck top of her dress.

"Oh, it's you!" cried Desiree in equal surprise, looking Lily up and down with more than usual curiosity.

"Yes," replied the other,

"What are you doing here?"

"I–"

Desiree got no further, for at that moment, Chad and Sandra both rushed into the kitchen, and stopped, eyes passing from each of the two women there, to each other, in complete bewilderment.

"What's going on here?" asked Chad and Sandra, simultaneously, and with equal tones of anger.

"Uh... you invited me here," replied Lily and Desiree at the same time, both trying to be helpful.

"WHAT?"

Chad strode angrily over towards Sandra, face reddening with anger as he growled,

"Working late, are you?"

"Oh, you too, huh?" spat Sandra.

"Why did you lie to me?"

"Oh, that's rich isn't it, coming from you!" Chad exploded, stepping closer to her, and Desiree and Lily shared an alarmed glance.

Desiree could sense what Lily was thinking, and at a tiny nod from the pale, green-eyed beauty she stepped forwards, breasts bouncing gently as she announced in her most enticing tones, "Maybe it would be best if we just all calmed down a little..."

"You stay out of this!" snapped Sandra, turning to her in fury, but Desiree, unfazed, merely blinked her sky-blue eyes innocently. "But Sandra, didn't you invite Lily here to have fun?" she asked coaxingly.

"I – well, I suppose so," admitted Sandra, defusing slightly.

She and Chad were both still too worked up to notice it odd that Desiree and Lily should already be on first-name terms.

"And I'm guessing that's why you invited me here, as well," added Desiree, turning to Chad and leaning towards him, so that he began breathing in the intoxicating, spicy scent of her skin.

"Well, yes," said Chad,

"But she –"

"It looks like we haven't all been exactly straight with each other," went on Desiree, in the same mesmerizing and soothing tones as before, "But since we are all here now, we might as well all enjoy it... don't you think?"

She looked from husband to wife, beaming at them as she took in their stunned expressions.

"I... what?" asked Sandra, and then fell silent, looking at Chad in some consternation.

He looked back, the same confused turmoil battling on his face, and all was quiet.

"I agree," said Lily suddenly, breaking the tension which had been building up and startling both Chad and Sandra considerably,

"Why shouldn't we all just enjoy each other?"

With a soft, fluid motion, she reached up to the buttons of her blouse, undoing them one by one as she slunk sultrily up to Chad.

"You, for one, look like you can show a girl a good time," she commented, flicking her hips from side to side as she opened her blouse in front of Chad, revealing her naked breasts, white as pearls.

Chad stared at these, still too confused to react, and Desiree responded instead, stepping closer to them and purring,

"Oh yes, he does, I can tell you..."

"Mmm, I bet you can as well, can't you?" asked Lily, turning to her, and Desiree, sliding with a cat-like grace, moved towards her, reaching up to untie the halter neck of her dress so that the red fabric fell away from her own tanned, round breasts, and coming to Lily, she began rubbing them on hers, moaning as they reached for one another, pressing their mouths together in a passionate kiss.

Chad and Sandra looked on, absolute astonishment flooding their veins.

"Is this really happening?" murmured Sandra wonderingly; the expectant twinge in her pussy sincerely hoping that it was.

"I don't know," replied Chad, reaching out to take her hand,

"But I like it..."

He squeezed her and she turned to him, all animosity is forgotten as she saw the delightful mischievousness gleaming in his eyes.

Lily and Desiree were still rubbing their breasts together, their tongues revolving in a mid-air kiss, and now, without stopping their oral activities, both turned their eyes to the watching pair in unambiguous invitation.

"Maybe it might be nice to join in," suggested Chad, reaching up to stroke a lock of Sandra's deep brown hair back from her face.

"Mmm," agreed Sandra, stepping closer to him, and rubbing her crotch rhythmically against him.

Lily and Desiree, breaking apart for a moment, slunk over to the couple, joining in as they began rubbing together, and slowly, almost in a trance, the four began peeling away each other's layers, the whole scene so dreamlike that neither Chad nor Sandra were quite aware of what had happened. Somehow, though, they very soon stood all four together entirely nude, and eagerly, Chad ushered them into the lounge, where the stereo was oozing syrupy melodies over a deep, throbbing beat. After entering they stood for a second, still getting used to the atmosphere, gazing at each other as they tried to take it all in.

The sight of three women, one a complete stranger (and a particularly beautiful one) standing naked in front of him in his own living room was awakening in Chad such a powerful lust that he sat down heavily on the couch, gazing from one to another of them in voracious indecision. Lily and Desiree, on entering, immediately began dancing to the music, swinging their hips snakily from side to side and flicking their long hair playfully about their shoulders.

Closer and closer to each other, they stepped, sticking their tongues out and wriggling them seductively on each other's mouths. Sandra stepped closer too, entranced by this scene, and Lily turned to her, circling her hips around until she was pressing her hot pussy on Sandra's. Gasping, the latter started also gyrating her hips, and then she moaned excitedly as Desiree joined in, so that all three were humping each other with long, throbbing flicks of their pelvises which were causing Chad to grip his shaft and begin fondling himself, feeling his hunger growing inexorably within him though he was still not yet quite ready to fully join in.

Lily's sweet juices were running down one of Sandra's thighs and Desiree's down her other, and unthinkingly she shot her hands out, connecting with both openings, the flesh so softly lovely she felt she was plunging her hands into two sweet, hot flowers, and she wriggled her fingers more, eager to get to the nectar.

Lily and Desiree started jerking their pussies back and forth on Sandra's fingers and she gasped, whole body thrilling with the intensely amazing sensation of stimulating two other women at once. Then suddenly the thrill increased infinitely, and looking down, she saw that Lily had begun running her fingers all around Sandra's entrance, vibrating them on her clitoris and running them up and down her mound of Venus with electrifying flicks.

The feelings being elicited in Sandra were so powerful now that she sank to the floor, Lily and Desiree joining her so that they were all kneeling, legs spread wide apart, as they continued fondling each other. They were just in front of Chad on the couch now and Desiree, who happened to be closest to him, twisted her head around, finding his engorged cock and engulfing it in her warm pink mouth as Sandra began dancing her fingers deeper and deeper inside her, increasing her speed as Lily started vibrating ever faster inside Sandra.

Humming in delight, Desiree began sliding her mouth up and down Chad's cock, flicking her tongue around the head with dizzying sensitivity, and he groaned, still moving his head from one to another of the women like a man at a buffet torn between too many choices. Desiree's mouth felt absolutely incredible around him; but the sight of Lily and Sandra pumping their fingers inside each other, while Sandra was continuing to fondle Desiree too at the same time, was turning him on more than he could bear.

"I have to fuck you, I have to fuck all of you!" he suddenly growled, and Desiree slid her mouth away from his cock, smiling up at saucily and then arching her spine as Sandra found her sweet spot and began playing with it.

Chad, still growling in hunger, pounced on Sandra, thrusting his cock into her alongside Lily's fingers so that Sandra gasped in wonder. The sensation was better than any vibrator she had ever tried, and she flung her legs wide, still pulsating her fingers wildly inside Lily and Desiree. She could feel Desiree bucking and jerking around on her, very close to climaxing, and cried out in anticipation, squeezing Chad and Lily deeper inside her as she started fingering Desiree with untamed gusto.

"Oh yes!" cried the blonde woman, lying back on the floor and tossing from side to side on Sandra's fingers, her pussy working crazily as her juices began pouring out of her.

The feeling of Desiree coming all over her hand was swiftly bringing on her own climax, aided greatly by Chad, who was now pumping his dick in and out of her so hard that Lily took her fingers away from Sandra's pussy to concentrate on the fantastic upwelling of sensations imbuing her. Looking up at Chad, she barely recognized the face of her husband, so incensed was he; and she lay back, still working her fingers manically inside Lily as she felt Chad penetrating her deeper than he ever had, pulling forth all of her strongest pleasures in one great wave; jerking her hips forward, she began screaming ecstatically as she felt the wave engulfing her, over and over again.

Chad grinned down at her, gasping at the sensation of her now super-sensitive pussy still gripping him. But he still felt compelled to move on, so he slid his dick from her, rolling over to Lily, who was bucking and writhing on Sandra's still-moving fingers. Chad began rubbing his cock around Lily's clitoris at the same time, and Sandra, seeing stars, slipped her fingers out, allowing Chad to slide right up inside Lily.

He gasped, gazing down at her in wonder, for a split second totally at a loss as reality crept in and all of his years of cultivated inhibitions told him how wrong it was to be fucking a total stranger, with whom he had not even exchanged a simple conversation, in front of two other people.

Then Lily winked at him, licking her velvety lips

appealingly, and he moved down, pressing his mouth to hers with deep desire. Raising his head again, he saw that Desiree and Sandra were lying, hands in each other's pussies, watching them with rapt attention. Lily flicked her hips, squeezing him inside her, and he growled, all qualms melting away as the deep throbbing wave of desire took him over again.

Lily, sensing him relax, began flicking her pelvis all around his dick, hugging him fantastically, and unable to contain himself any longer, he began fucking her, harder and harder; every yelp of delight she was emitting encouraging him to higher and higher states, and as she spread her legs even wider, inviting him deep into her core, he felt the wave surge up all around him, and gripping her small creamy ass, he started pounding her in a frenzy, exploding into her so fiercely that she immediately began coming as well, moaning in delight.

Rolling off her, Chad fell into the arms of Sandra, and all four began rolling together stickily on the floor, blissed out with rapturous joy.

Sometime later (no one had any idea how much), as they still lay naked on the floor, Desiree flicked her eyes towards Lily questioningly. The latter, understanding at once, gave a swift nod, and Desiree raised her head, beaming widely at the Joneses.

"I think you two are ready," she said happily, sitting up.

Lily sat up too, also smiling in a distinctly mischievous way, and Chad and Sandra looked from one to the other, bewilderment once more clouding their faces.

"For...what?" asked Sandra.

Desiree turned to her, stroking with one finger her clitoris and making her cry out in ecstasy.

"To fulfill all of your wildest dreams," she said simply. "Come with us."

"What?" asked Chad and Sandra, as the two women began making their way to the other room to pull their clothes on.

"It's better not to explain now," said Desiree, "We'll see when we get there."

"Get where?"

"The place we are going," said Desiree simply. "It's not far away. And you guys are going to love it there."

"Desiree, what are you talking about?" questioned Sandra insistently, but the younger woman silenced her by bringing a finger to her lips.

"Do you trust me?" she whispered.

"I...suppose so" –

"Then let's go."

Mystified, yet also thrilling with anticipation, they hastily donned their clothes and followed her out into the night.

She led them through some winding streets and down a number of back alleys which Chad and Sandra were not familiar with. Lily did seem to be, however; and for the first time since he had met her, Chad began wondering at the intense familiarity, which she and Desiree had been displaying all evening.

He did not have time to wonder much, however, for Desiree pausing in front of him showed that they had reached their destination. Looking up, he saw that they were at the door of a large, detached, white-painted house. Bending, Desiree pulled the top part of her dress away, revealing one caramel-colored nipple, which she pressed into some kind of receptacle in the door, which instantly swung open.

Turning to Chad and Sandra with a grin, her nipple still showing cheekily next to the blood-red material of her dress, she said, "Welcome."

Taking both of them by the hand, she led them through the doorway, Lily following comfortably. Chad and Sandra gasped as they saw that they were in a vast hall, hung about with brightly colored drapes, and filled with so many unusual objects that they could barely comprehend it. One thing was immediately apparent: everything here was to do with sex, from the marble pyramid of vibrators at Sandra's elbow to the handcuffs and whips which were fixed at regular intervals to the walls.

Off to their left and right were various doors, some closed and some slightly ajar, lending a titillating peek into the treasures which lay beyond. Standing in front of one of these doors was an entirely naked man who was standing before a camera, clearly totally engrossed in whatever he was filming in the room beyond.

"What is this place?" asked Chad, as the man greeted Lily and Desiree like old friends.

"This is the House of a Thousand Pleasures," explained the man with a grin. "Feel free to please yourself!"

"What do you mean?" asked Sandra incredulously.

Lily and Desiree stepped forwards, each taking one of her arms and stroking her.

"Whatever desires you have, however outlandish they seem," began Desiree,

"Or whatever preferences you have for how people should act, or what places should look like, that will really turn you on," added Lily. "Here you can enjoy fulfilling every one of them."

"You mean," asked Chad, who had been peeping into

some of the rooms, and was now quite breathless with anticipation. "Every room here has things in for us to play with?"

"Exactly," smiled Desiree, and Lily added,

"People too."

"Take your pick."

Chad and Sandra looked around, momentarily stunned. Up until about half an hour ago, they had felt that the activities of that night were the strangest and most explorative either would ever be involved in.

Now, however, as they glanced around at the numerous different worlds being offered in every room, and the three people smiling welcomingly at them, they began to realize the full scope of what their imaginations could offer, if they wanted.

Holding each other's hands, they plunged into the house.

ABOUT THE AUTHOR

Helana Parkins is an emerging erotica author of many erotica kinks and sub-genres. Be sure to check out other books and leave a review if this story got you hot!

Visit my blog at Helana Parkins Blog

Join my newsletter for exclusive previews Helana Parkins Newsletter

Sign up for Free Stories from Xplicit Press Authors

Xplicit Press Author Updates

Like Xplicit Press on Facebook

Follow Xplicit Press on Twitter

Readers: I want to expand a few of the stories to see where the characters can be explored further. If there are any of the stories that you would like to read more about again, I'd love to hear from you!

Keep In Touch
Helana Parkins
info@helanaparkins.com